Setup

Made in Savannah
Cozy Mystery Series Book Seven

Hope Callaghan

***

hopecallaghan.com

Visit my website for new releases and special offers: hopecallaghan.com

i

Thank you to these wonderful ladies who help make my books shine - Peggy H., Cindi G., Jean P., Wanda D. and Barbara W. for taking the time to preview *Setup in Savannah,* for the extra sets of eyes and for catching all of my mistakes.

A special thanks to my reader review team: Alice, Amary, Barbara, Becky, Becky B, Brinda, Cassie, Christina, Cyndi, Debbie, Denota, Devan, Grace, Jan, Jo-Ann, Joeline, Joyce, Jean K., Jean M., Kathy, Lynne, Megan, Melda, Kat, Linda, Lynne, Pat, Patsy, Paula, Renate, Rita, Rita P, Shelba, Tamara, Valerie and Vicki.

CONTENTS

Cast of Characters

Carlita Garlucci. The widow of a mafia "made" man, Carlita promised her husband on his deathbed to get their sons out of the "family" business, so she moves from New York to the historic city of Savannah, Georgia. But escaping the family isn't as easy as she hoped it would be and trouble follows Carlita to her new home.

Mercedes Garlucci. Carlita's daughter and the first to move to Savannah with her mother. An aspiring writer, Mercedes has a knack for finding mysteries and adventure.

Vincent Garlucci, Jr. Carlita's oldest son and a younger version of his father, Vinnie is deeply entrenched in the "family business" and is not interested in leaving New York.

Tony Garlucci. Carlita's middle son and the first to follow his mother to Savannah. Tony is protective of both his mother and his sister, which is a good thing since the Garlucci women are always in some sort of a predicament.

Paulie Garlucci. Carlita's youngest son. Mayor of the small town of Clifton Falls, NY, Paulie never joined the "family business," and is content to live his life with his wife and young children far away from a life of crime. Gina, Paulie's wife, rules the family household with an iron fist.

Chapter 1

Mercedes Garlucci picked up the pace and hurried across the street to Savannah's historic riverfront district.

Despite it being early fall, a warm breeze blew off the Savannah River and Mercedes impatiently swiped her hair from her eyes. She warily kept her eyes on the dark corners of the towering buildings surrounding her, and let out a yelp as she stumbled on one of the loose cobblestones that formed the historic city street.

For the umpteenth time, Mercedes wondered why she had agreed to meet the mysterious author, Jon Luis, near the creepy old warehouse.

A small *ping* noise echoed from the alley behind the sprawling Artisan Hotel, and the pungent odor of rotting fish filled the night air.

She slowed her pace as she rounded the side of the building and let out the breath she was holding when the bright streetlights illuminated the riverfront walkway. At least she wasn't meeting Jon Luis in some dark alley, although, technically, this wasn't much better.

The promise of an inside scoop on a decades-old murder case, The Madison Square murder, had been too tempting. Mercedes was fascinated with the story of old Georgia money and greed. The fact that some of the people involved once held prominent positions in Savannah deepened the mystery.

Mercedes hoped to do a little "sleuthing" and get her hands on some insider information for her new murder mystery novel, *Savannah's Secret Society*. Her plan was for the new novel to tie in with the mafia, something Mercedes was all too familiar with.

Mercedes jumped at the tinkling of laughter echoing from one the Artisan's upper balconies.

She cast a quick glance toward the building before stepping onto the sidewalk out front. Luis' last message directed her to make her way past the Artisan, where she would find a fountain and a display of a bronze tall-ship.

"Turn left," she muttered under her breath. "Where is he taking me?" She carefully navigated the uneven brick street and briefly wondered what was worse...the cobblestone streets or the old bricks, which were literally stumbling blocks.

Finally, Mercedes reached the corner and the parking lot adjacent to the last string of shops in the tourist district. She peered to the left of the parking lot, at a large industrial building with smoke billowing out of the smokestacks. *Private Lot B*. "This is it."

She tiptoed along the edge of the parking lot until she was standing directly under a cluster of trees that lined the riverbank. "Jon Luis?" she hissed. "It's me. Mercedes Garlucci." There was no answer, so she circled the tree, stepping closer to the fence when she nearly tripped over something lying on the ground.

Mercedes shuffled to the right, attempting to ease around what she thought was a tree root and her pulse quickened when she realized it was a man, sprawled out on the ground.

"Hello?" Mercedes nudged the man with the tip of her shoe. "Hey."

Mercedes stuck her fingers in her mouth and let out a low whistle, the signal to her friend, Autumn, who was trailing close behind and keeping a watchful eye on Mercedes, that she needed her.

Autumn flew around the side of the tree, her gun drawn and her eyes darting wildly.

"Oh my gosh! Autumn. Watch where you point that thing!" Mercedes jumped back and out of Autumn's firing range.

"Sorry." Autumn eased her stance. "You were only supposed to call me in an emergency, so I assumed it was weapon-worthy."

"It might be. I guess I shoulda brought my gun." Mercedes pointed at the man lying on the ground next to the tree. "I'm not sure if this is a homeless person or my contact, Jon Luis."

Autumn whipped a flashlight out of her back pocket, clicked it on and scanned the man's body. "Uh-oh. See that?" She focused the light near the man's head and Mercedes spotted a pool of blood.

"We need an ambulance." Mercedes' fingers trembled as she pulled her cell phone from her back pocket, switched it on and dialed 911. "Yes. My name is Mercedes Garlucci. I'm over in the riverfront district, not far from the Artisan Hotel and there's a man lying on the ground next to the parking lot. There's some blood near his head and he's not responding. You need my exact location? Hang on."

She hurried to the front of the parking lot. "I'm in Private Lot B, on West River Street, past the edge of the shopping area. Thank you."

Mercedes made her way back to Autumn's side as she disconnected the line. "The police are on the way."

"Is this the dude you were supposed to meet?"

"I-I don't know." Mercedes swallowed hard and took a step closer to study his face. She'd never met Jon Luis, but had talked to him on the phone. They had also exchanged numerous text and email messages.

At first, Mercedes wondered if "Jon Luis" was a scammer, but she'd done some digging around and discovered the man had written a series of books about several high profile unsolved murders.

She and her author group had discussed Mr. Luis' books at length, and when Mercedes decided to dig a little deeper into Luis' life, she was convinced she was onto something. Why the man had agreed to meet with Mercedes to discuss the scandalous stories of some of Savannah's most powerful people was a mystery.

She studied his face, his receding hairline and gray beard. The man appeared to be close to Jon Luis' age. His glasses hung haphazardly from his nose and a set of keys lay close by. Mercedes reached out to grab the keys.

"Don't touch that!" Autumn said. "You could be contaminating evidence. I'll take a picture instead." Autumn tucked her gun in the front of her waistband and pulled her shirt over the top before dropping to her knees. She positioned her phone over the set of keys and snapped a picture.

Next, she scooched back and snapped a picture of the deceased before hurrying to the edge of the parking lot to take a few more pictures.

The sound of sirens filled the air and flashes of light filled River Street. Several patrol cars, along with an ambulance, arrived en masse and uniformed officers swarmed the scene.

"Over here." Mercedes led the officers to the man's body and then joined Autumn, who stood off to the side. They watched as the emergency medical responders and police examined the man Mercedes believed was Jon Luis.

One of the officers made his way over. "You two the ones who found the man?"

"I was," Mercedes said.

"Do you know who he is?" he asked.

"No sir. I mean, I've never met the man. If he's who I think he is, I was meeting him here tonight," Mercedes started to ramble. "I believe his name might be Jon Luis. I didn't know him and my friend, Autumn, was waiting for me across the street."

"Stay here. I'll be right back." The officer made his way to one of the patrol cars and returned, carrying a notepad. "You say you were here to meet the deceased, but yet you didn't know him."

"It's a little complicated," Mercedes said. "I came here to meet a man by the name of Jon Luis. I've seen pictures of him and I think this may be the man on the ground. Of course, it's dark, so I can't be certain. He was going to give me information on an old unsolved murder investigation because I'm writing a book about Savannah's dark side; you know crimes, murder..." Her voice trailed off.

"So you agreed to meet a complete stranger, at night, in a dark parking lot to get the scoop on an unsolved murder and when you got here you found a body?"

"That about sums it up," Mercedes said. "Listen, no one can make up this kind of story."

"I wouldn't be so sure." The officer rocked back on his heels. "I would like you." He pointed his finger at Mercedes and Autumn. "Both of you, to accompany me to the police station to answer a few questions."

Mercedes cleared her throat. "Okay."

The officer reached for his radio while Autumn grabbed Mercedes' arm and whispered in her ear. "Don't say anything else. I'm gonna tell him we want a lawyer present for questioning."

"We're not being arrested," Mercedes said. "Are we?"

The officer glanced at the women as he spoke to the dispatcher. "10-4. We'll be leaving shortly." He clipped his radio to his belt. "My patrol car is parked over here."

"Wait." Autumn held up her hand. "We would rather answer your questions here. Why do we have to go down to the police station?"

"You don't. I thought it would be easier to talk down at the station but I can't force you."

"Then we're not going anywhere." Autumn crossed her arms and her shirt bunched up, revealing the grip of her gun.

"You're carrying a concealed weapon?" The officer narrowed his eyes and pointed at her gun.

"I-uh." Autumn uncrossed her arms. "Yes. For protection. I have a weapons license."

"Can I see your driver's license and carry license?"

"Of course." Autumn fumbled around inside her jacket pocket and pulled out a small wallet. She unclasped the front, removed her carry license and driver's license, and then handed them to the officer.

He glanced at the front. "I'll be right back."

"Great," Mercedes moaned as the officer strode to his patrol car. "Now I'm sure they're gonna arrest us and haul us down to the station."

"How can they?" Autumn asked. "We haven't done anything wrong. I mean, sure it doesn't look good meeting a total stranger at night, in a remote area, he may be dead and I'm carrying a loaded gun."

"Maybe he's just unconscious," Mercedes said. "I better call Ma to let her know there's a chance we're on our way to jail."

***

Carlita Garlucci hummed as she rearranged the array of flatbreads. Soon, Paulie, Carlita's youngest son, would return with Gina and the kids.

Gina had originally planned to fly down the previous Saturday, but the triplets, Carlita's grandchildren, had all come down with colds and Gina wanted to wait until they were feeling better.

She managed to find a last minute flight into the Hilton Head / Savannah Regional Airport, and although it would be late by the time they arrived, Carlita thought they could at least munch on a quick snack and spend a few minutes catching up before heading off to bed.

It would be Gina's first visit to Savannah and Carlita wanted everything to be perfect. She hoped her daughter-in-law would fall in love with

Savannah and love it so much; she would head back to Clifton Falls, New York, pack her bags and the family would move south.

Carlita was trying not to get her hopes up. Gina was born and raised in New York. It was her home. Her parents lived there. Her siblings lived there. Paulie was mayor of Clifton Falls and had a promising career in politics.

"Perfect." Carlita placed the potholder inside the drawer and pulled her apron off. She had the whole week planned for the family. While Gina and Paulie spent time alone, patching things up after Gina practically kicked her husband out of the house, she would spend time with Gracie, Noel and Paulie, Jr. or "PJ" for short.

They would visit the children's museum, the wildlife center and spend some time at Forsyth Park, which sported two large children's playgrounds. High on her list was a trip to the famous Leopold's Ice Cream for some sweet treats.

She glanced worriedly out the window at the darkening skies. Mercedes had gone out earlier, vaguely mentioning meeting a contact to discuss an old Savannah murder mystery she planned to use in an upcoming novel.

When pressed for details, Mercedes told her mother she was meeting a fellow author, Jon Luis, a man who knew a great deal about the colorful characters and rich residents of Savannah. She assured her mother it was perfectly safe, that she'd done a thorough background check on Mr. Luis and he was on the up and up. Just to be safe, she'd asked Autumn to go with her.

Rambo, Carlita's pooch, trotted through his doggie door and Carlita followed him out onto the deck. She placed both elbows on the railing and breathed deeply. Her thoughts wandered to Gina and Paulie again. She couldn't wait for her daughter-in-law to meet Shelby and Violet, to meet Cool Bones, another one of the tenants who lived in her apartment building.

Carlita frowned as she thought about her other tenant, Elvira Cobb. The woman was trouble with a capital "T." She'd nearly gotten herself killed during a recent investigation, and if it hadn't been for Carlita and her children, she would likely be six foot under.

"What on earth is keeping Mercedes? I better find out what's going on," she told Rambo, and then headed back inside the apartment.

It took a few minutes for Carlita to remember where she'd left her cell phone. When she picked it up, she noticed she'd not only missed a call from her daughter, but the volume on her phone was turned down.

She turned the volume up and then dialed Mercedes' cell phone.

"Hey Ma. I tried calling you," Mercedes said.

"I had the volume turned down. I was gettin' worried about you. You on your way home?"

"I don't know," Mercedes said. "I got to the spot where I was supposed to meet Jon Luis and found some guy lying on the ground and unresponsive, so Autumn and I called the police."

"Is...he gonna be all right?"

"No. The cops just told us he's dead."

Chapter 2

Carlita tightened her grip on her cell phone. "Where are ya? I'm gonna come down there."

"I'm at the end of West River Street, near the last of the tourist shops," Mercedes said. "We're in the end parking lot, right next to the creepy factory on the river. You can't miss it. The place is swarming with cops."

"I'll be there in a few minutes," Carlita said. "Don't say nothin' else to the cops until I get there."

"Autumn and I already agreed we're going to insist on having an attorney present for questioning."

Carlita told Mercedes that she was on her way and then hurried to her bedroom to grab a sweater and her purse.

She was halfway to the front door when it swung open and her middle son, Tony, stepped inside. "I closed up shop. Paulie called. Him, Gina and the kids are about ten minutes away."

"You're gonna have to hang out here and hold down the fort to wait for them." Carlita shifted her purse to her other arm. "Mercedes was supposed to meet some guy down by the riverfront, to interview him for her new book. When she got there, she found a body and called the cops."

"Was it the guy she was supposed to meet?"

"She thinks so," Carlita said. "I'm headin' down there now."

"Tell her not to talk to the cops," Tony said. "Don't let her take the heat, neither. The cops'll try to coerce a confession."

"How do you know so much about this?" Carlita waved her hand. "Never mind. I don't wanna know. I'll call you as soon as I know what's goin' on."

Tony accompanied his mother out of the apartment building and walked her to her car.

She gave him a quick hug. "We might need to scrape together some bond money."

"I hope not." Two bright beams of light flashed across the parking lot as a car pulled into the alley. It was Paulie's car. "I better say hello to Gina and the kids." Carlita waited until Paulie steered the car into an empty spot before she hurried to the passenger side of the car.

The door opened and a petite, slender dark-haired woman stepped out.

"Gina. I'm glad you're here. Welcome to Savannah." Carlita gave her daughter-in-law a warm hug, keeping both hands on Gina's arms as she took a step back. "I love what you've done to your hair."

Gina ran her fingers through her shoulder length locks. "Thanks. I was gonna cut it a little shorter." She shrugged. "Paulie likes it long."

The back door of the sedan flew open. A small child hopped out and flung himself at Carlita's legs. "Nonna."

Carlita bent down and picked up her son's namesake, Paulie. "Oh my PJ. I think you've grown a whole foot since Nonna saw you last."

Another child, Carlita's granddaughter, Gracie, sprang from the car and ran to her grandmother's side. "PJ is in trouble."

"So are you," PJ insisted. "Mommy said we're all in trouble."

Noel slipped out of the car and joined her siblings. "I'm hungry."

"I know you are." Gina shook her head. "It was the longest four hours of my life and I will never endure a long layover with these three again. I shoulda made Paulie come get us."

Paulie exited the car. "I offered to come get ya."

Gina ignored the comment and gazed at the back of the apartment building. "This is your building? The way Paulie described it; I was expectin' the Taj Mahal."

Carlita could tell from the tone of Gina's voice that she wasn't impressed with their home.

"You're lookin' at the back of the building." Paulie popped the trunk, reached inside and grabbed a suitcase. "Give it a chance, Gina."

"I have some snacks in the apartment and juice for the kids." Carlita jingled her car keys. "I gotta take care of somethin' for Mercedes." She shot Tony a warning glance and he nodded. The last thing Carlita needed was for Gina to start ranting and raving about what a dangerous place Savannah was after hearing Mercedes was at a potential crime scene.

She hugged her grandchildren and Gina one more time and waited until they disappeared inside the apartment before climbing into her car and backing out of the parking spot. It was a short ten-minute walk to the riverfront district, but it was dark and since she was alone, Carlita decided to drive.

On top of that, she wasn't sure if she would have to follow Mercedes and Autumn to the police station if they were taken in for questioning. Carlita wondered if Detective Zachary Jackson was on the scene. He and Mercedes had been dating. Well, not technically dating...they'd gone on one date.

She turned onto Bay Street and drove to the other side of the Riverfront District. When she reached the Artisan Hotel, she turned right, onto a bumpy cobblestone street.

The ruts jostled Carlita as the car crept along the uneven roadway. When she stopped at the bottom of the hill, she spied the flashing lights of the patrol cars and figured she was close.

After a quick left turn onto River Street, she pulled into the parking lot marked Private Lot B, slid out of the car and joined the crowd that had gathered.

Carlita circled the onlookers until she caught a glimpse of her daughter and Autumn standing off to the side, talking with a police officer.

"...and I swear that is all I know. I've never met the man before in my life. I know it sounds odd."

"You don't have to talk Mercedes." Carlita eased in between Autumn and Mercedes, and squeezed her daughter's arm.

The uniformed officer lifted a brow. "And who are you?"

"Mercedes' mother." Carlita lifted her chin defiantly. "Who are you?"

"I'm Detective Skip Wilson." The man clicked the end of his pen as he studied Carlita's face. "You have a unique name. What's your last name again?" The detective consulted his notes. "Garlucci. You wouldn't happen to know a Detective Zachary Jackson, would you?"

"We're, uh, friends," Mercedes said. "He helped us track down one of our tenants who went missing not long ago."

The detective smirked. "Ah, now I remember. There was some nut job woman who was camped out at Fort Pulaski and ended up being kidnapped by a killer."

"My tenant, Elvira Cobb," Carlita said. "Please don't hold it against us."

"I think I've got enough information to go on for now. You're free to leave." The detective fished a business card out of his front shirt pocket and handed it to Mercedes. "If you think of anything you forgot to mention, give me a call."

"I will." Mercedes took the card, and the trio waited until the detective made his way over to the crime scene investigators.

"What happened, Mercedes?"

"Like I told you earlier, my author group and I were discussing, Jon Luis, a famous local author.

He wrote a book about an unsolved murder back in the early 1980s involving several prominent, local Savannah residents. It seemed like such an interesting story and it gave me an idea to start a new book, *Savannah's Secret Society,* so I contacted Mr. Luis. We emailed, texted back and forth and finally set up a time to meet."

Mercedes went on to tell her mother Jon Luis refused to meet in a public place and insisted they meet at night. "He picked this location. I jumped at the chance to meet with him, but then I got to thinking it was dangerous to meet a stranger alone at night."

"So Mercedes asked me to tag along," Autumn said. "The plan was for me to stay out of sight so we wouldn't spook the guy."

"I almost didn't recognize you." Carlita pointed at Autumn's ball cap, black t-shirt and matching sweatpants.

"I was keeping a low profile." Autumn patted her pistol, still tucked under her shirt. "Don't worry, we were both protected."

Carlita's eyes widened. "You brought a gun? Do the cops know you have a gun?"

"Yeah; I have a carry license, so they cleared me." Autumn tapped the tip of her black sneaker on the ground. "While Mercedes was talking to the cop, I wandered closer to the scene. From what the investigators were saying, it looks like the man was shot from behind. He never even saw it coming."

"Poor thing." Carlita made a cross symbol across her chest and then glanced behind her. "I parked the car over there. Where are your Segways?"

"They're up on the hill. We left them locked up next to the bike racks," Mercedes said. "I was hoping to meet with Jon Luis and be back home before Gina and the kids showed up."

"Too late." Carlita, Mercedes and Autumn slowly walked to the front of the parking lot. "They got to the apartment just as I was leaving. I didn't tell them what happened. I don't want Gina to get the wrong impression of Savannah." She motioned towards the hill. "I'll give you a ride back to the Segways."

"That's probably not a bad idea." Mercedes shivered as she glanced at the team of crime scene investigators. "The killer could still be lurking nearby."

The women climbed into the back seat while Carlita slid behind the wheel. She slowly drove out of the parking lot, up the hill and stopped in front of the bike rack. "Do you want me to follow you home?"

"No." Mercedes opened the car door. "This touristy area is safe and there are still a lot of people out. I'm sure we'll be okay to make it home on our own."

"Thanks for the ride Mrs. G." Autumn slid out of the seat and stepped onto the sidewalk. "I'll have to swing by to meet the rest of your family. Is Vinnie coming down here for a visit anytime soon?"

Carlita had detected a spark between Autumn and her oldest son, Vinnie, during his last visit. "He promised me that he'll be here for Thanksgiving."

"I've been wondering how he's been." Autumn smiled at Carlita and slowly closed the door.

Carlita waited until the women slipped their helmets on and were on their way before pulling onto the main street.

During the drive home, she thought about her family, how she had vowed to her husband on his deathbed that she would get their sons out of the "family business."

Her hope was that a move to Savannah would give them all a fresh start, a chance to start over again. Despite her best efforts, parts of Carlita's past life had followed them from Queens all the way to their new home.

Tony seemed happy with his new life in Savannah, even thriving since he started dating Shelby Towns, one of Carlita's tenants. He was also doing a wonderful job of running their pawnshop, *Savannah Swag*.

When Paulie came to visit after his argument with Gina, Carlita hoped the charm of the historic city, not to mention the wonderful weather and tons of fun things to do, would be tempting enough for him to consider moving.

Gina, on the other hand, would be a tough sell, which is why Carlita had worked hard to plan every single detail of Gina and the children's visit, in hopes of letting her see for herself what she was missing.

Then there was Vinnie. He was the first of her sons to visit Savannah. He'd shown an interest in Autumn and Carlita thought there was a possibility he would consider moving south, but

Vinnie was firmly entrenched in the "family business."

She hoped, over time, he would come to see how dangerous the mafia life was, see that his brother was happy living in Savannah and would change his mind. Whether "the family" would let him leave...that was another matter. There was a famous saying in La Cosa Nostra...*The only way you leave the family is in a box.*

It was Carlita's greatest fear Vinnie wouldn't make it out and she would end up burying her beloved son like she had his father.

Mercedes and Autumn must have taken a shortcut because by the time Carlita parked the car and made her way to the back of the apartment building, Mercedes was already there.

"Where's Autumn?"

"I dropped her off at *Shades of Ink*. Steve was closing up shop and she wanted to wait for him."

"Have you met Steve's girlfriend?" Carlita asked.

"Paisley? Yeah. She and Steve met at a tattoo conference or something like that." Mercedes unlocked the back door and steered her Segway into the hall. "Did you know that Paisley has over a hundred tattoos?"

"I wouldn't be surprised," Carlita murmured. She waited while her daughter hung her helmet on the Segway's handlebar before climbing the stairs and making their way into the apartment.

Carlita's grandchildren were sprawled out on the living room floor watching television while Tony, Paulie and Gina were seated at the dining room table.

Paulie turned. "Everything okay?"

"Yeah...uh." Mercedes shot her mother a quick glance. "I was having a little trouble with my Segway, so Ma drove over to help out," she fibbed.

"Segways sound fun." Paulie glanced at his wife.

"They sound dangerous," Gina turned to Carlita. "I brought you a couple bags of your favorite bagels from Blumenthal's. I thought we could have 'em for breakfast. They're down in my suitcase."

Paulie, Gina and the kids were staying in Tony's downstairs apartment while Tony camped out on Carlita's sofa bed.

"I'll go get them," Paulie said.

Gina waved her hand. "Nah. They're packed away and you'll never find them. It'll only take me a second."

"I left Tony's apartment door unlocked," Paulie said.

"I'll be right back." Gina hurried out of the apartment, leaving the door ajar.

Carlita waited until she heard the click of her heels on the stairs before turning to her youngest son. "How's it goin'?"

Paulie shrugged. "It's hard to tell with Gina. She's cranky cuz of her havin' to deal with the kids and the layover at the airport. I probably won't know until tomorrow. At least she's not insisting I take her back to the airport."

"True." Carlita picked up a slice of the rustic Italian flatbread and bit the end. The pungent aroma of fresh basil wafted up. "I think these would've been better if I woulda added a layer of pesto."

"They're perfect the way they are, Ma," Tony said. "Did you want to talk to Gina about havin' a small dinner party and invitin' Shelby and Violet?"

"Of course. I think that would be nice." She started to tell them what she planned to serve when a commotion out in the hallway interrupted the conversation.

"Well, I don't know who you think you are, but you can take your New York attitude right on back there!"

Chapter 3

"Uh-oh," Carlita said. "I think Gina and Elvira just met." She sprang from the chair and darted out into the hallway where Gina and Elvira stood glaring at each other at the top of the stairs. "What's going on?"

"This..." Elvira waved her hands wildly. "Buttinsky told me I can't leave my easel down in the hallway." She lowered her voice, "Because it's in her way," Elvira said, nearly nailing Gina's nasally voice.

Carlita covered her mouth to hide the grin. She'd suspected Gina and Elvira would clash and it appeared she was correct. "I'm sorry if Elvira's easel is in your way." She turned to her tenant. "Perhaps we can put it in front of the storage closet instead."

"Why?" Elvira clenched her fists. "Is it gonna kill her to take two more steps to walk around it?"

"Elvira," Carlita soothed. "This is a non-issue. I'm sure Gina is concerned one of her children will trip over it or that they might knock it over and bust it." The explanation sounded plausible to Carlita.

"Promise me this woman isn't moving into the building and I'll move it," Elvira said.

"She's not moving in," Carlita said.

"Fine. I'll move it." Elvira stomped down the steps, picked up the easel and dropped it in front of the closet door before stomping back up. "I hope you're happy."

"Infinitely," Gina smiled smugly, and when Elvira shot her a dirty look, Gina gave Elvira's back the one-finger salute as she marched to her apartment door.

Elvira turned back once and scowled at them before stepping inside her apartment and slamming the door shut.

The pictures on the hall wall rattled.

Gina curled her lip. "What a piece of trash. Whatcha' doin' letting nasty people like her live here? I'm half tempted to move in just to tick her off."

Carlita followed Gina into the apartment and quietly closed the door behind them. "That would set off some fireworks."

"I see Gina met Elvira," Tony said. "Better up our liability insurance before those two get into a knockdown drag out fight and someone gets hurt."

Gina flicked her wrist and studied her fingernails. "All I can say is she better not mess with Gina Garlucci. She's more than met her match. The woman got me so ticked off, I forgot about the bagels."

"I'll get them." Paulie sprang from his chair. He exited the apartment, returning a short time later with three bags of bagels.

Gracie wandered to her father's side. She began rubbing her eyes and pressed her head against his leg. "My tummy hurts."

Paulie picked her up. "We should get the kids to bed," he told his wife.

"Yeah. It's been a long day." Gina gathered the other two children while Paulie thanked Tony for letting them use his apartment for the next few days.

After they were gone, Tony helped his mother pull out the sleeper sofa.

"Thanks for bein' such a good sport about letting Paulie and them use your apartment."

"No problem, Ma. Don't be gettin' your hopes up too high that Gina's gonna wanna move down here."

"I'm trying not to."

Mercedes carried an armful of pillows into the living room and tossed them on top of the bed.

"What happened to the guy down by the river?" Tony asked. "Was it the one you were supposed to meet?"

"Yeah. Someone shot him." Mercedes told her brother the story, how she'd been talking to Jon Luis, a well-known local author, about an old murder investigation and how they'd planned to meet down by the river that evening. "Like I told Ma, it was kinda weird because he didn't want to meet in a public place or during the day."

"And he just happened to get clipped right before he met you," Tony said. "Anybody else know about the meetin'?"

"Now that you mention it, the other authors in my group knew. We were all excited about it because we figured he had an inside scoop about an old, high profile unsolved murder case."

"You need to tell the police," Carlita said, "so they can check it out."

"Yeah," Tony agreed. "Seems suspicious to me that he died the same night of your meeting and others knew about it."

"I'll call Detective Wilson first thing in the morning." Mercedes lifted both hands over her head and stretched her back. "Right now, I'm beat."

Carlita wasn't far behind her daughter and turned in a short time later. It had been a long day, or more precisely, a long evening. She lay there for a long time, wondering if Gina and Paulie had patched things up.

She was excited to spend time with her grandchildren and mentally ticked off the list of fun things she had planned.

Her mind wandered to Jon Luis, the man Mercedes had planned to meet. What if Mercedes had arrived at the meeting spot early and ran into the killer? Even with a pistol-packing Autumn close by, the killer could've easily shot Mercedes before Autumn was able to reach her.

Carlita made a mental note to remind Mercedes to contact Detective Wilson the next morning and share the fact the other authors in her group knew about the planned meeting.

What if someone had it in for Jon Luis and the person was desperate to keep him from talking to Mercedes? If that was the case, was Mercedes' life in danger? Carlita's stomach churned at the thought.

Somehow, she had to convince her daughter to bow out of the author group, or at least avoid them until the authorities tracked down Jon Luis' killer.

Her last thought as she drifted off to sleep was the confrontation between Elvira and Gina. It was going to be a long week, especially if the two of them continued to cross paths. She couldn't think of two more bullheaded people than her troublesome tenant and daughter-in-law.

Carlita was the first one up the next morning and she tiptoed through the living room to the kitchen to start a pot of coffee. Although she tried to keep quiet, Tony started to stir and finally crawled out of bed.

"You gotta do somethin' about the metal bar on the sofa bed." He rubbed his back. "It felt like I was sleepin' on a tire jack."

"I'm sorry son. I had no idea it was so uncomfortable. Of course, I've never slept on it." Carlita poured water in the back of the coffee maker and turned it on. "You wanna Blumenthal bagel?"

"Sure." He stepped into the kitchen to help his mother fix the bagels and after they finished toasting, Carlita slathered a thick layer of cream cheese on them while Tony poured two cups of coffee. They carried the bagels and coffee out onto the balcony.

The early morning air was cool and crisp and Carlita shivered. "I need my sweater." She hurried inside, grabbed her sweater off the chair and headed back to the deck. "I'm sorry about the bed. I got an air mattress around here somewhere. We can put it on top of the mattress."

They sat on the deck, chatting about the pawnshop business, Gina and Paulie's visit and finally, the death of Jon Luis. "I'm thinkin' the people in Mercedes' author group need to be questioned," Carlita said.

"Yeah, you're probably right. Time for a refill." Tony carried their empty coffee cups back inside while Carlita and Rambo stayed on the deck.

Tony returned with the coffee and Mercedes trailing behind.

"You're up early." Carlita took the coffee cup from her son.

"I couldn't sleep." Mercedes eased into an empty chair. "I kept thinkin' about Jon Luis, wondering how long he'd been there and how if I woulda been there a few minutes earlier, I mighta been a witness to his murder."

Tony sipped his coffee. "Didja notice anyone hanging around while you were waitin' on the cops to show up?"

"No, but now that you mention it, Autumn and I noticed a set of keys near his body. She took a few pictures and sent them to me. I'll go get my phone." Mercedes headed back inside and returned with her cell phone.

She switched her phone on and clicked on the camera icon before scrolling through the screen. "Here they are." She handed the phone to her brother.

Tony tapped the screen to enlarge the picture. "Looks like a buncha keys. He was probably holdin' onto 'em when he got whacked and dropped 'em on the way down." He handed the phone to his mother.

Carlita squinted her eyes and studied the photo. "Looks like car keys and house keys...but there is one that looks different." She handed the phone to her daughter. "It's the one with a plastic key tag."

"You're right," Mercedes said. "I have no idea what it is." She switched the phone off and set it on the table. "I hope they track down the killer soon. This whole thing is creepin' me out."

"You think someone in your writing group might be a suspect?" Carlita asked.

"I hate to think of any of them as suspects."
Mercedes rattled off the names of the other
authors. "There's Tom Muldoon. He's gotta be
in his 50s. Tom writes thriller/suspense novels
and lives out of town. He's kinda quiet."

"Then there's Stephanie Rumsfield. She's
older, a throwback from the hippie era.
Stephanie writes Harlequin-type romance."
Mercedes wrinkled her nose. "She moved here
from Montana with her boyfriend."

Mercedes told them the third was Cricket
Tidwell. "She's sweet as can be and writes
crochet and cook books. She owns *The Book
Nook* and lives above the store."

"What about the young guy, the one you met
for coffee a few weeks back?" Carlita asked.

"Austin Crawford? Austin writes historical
mysteries set in the Civil War era. His dad is
an author, too. I forget his name."

"All four of them knew you were meetin'
with this Jon Luis guy last night?" Tony asked.

"Yeah. I mean. It's kind of a big deal. Jon Luis is…was famous around these parts. Snagging an interview with him is unheard of," Mercedes said.

"You need to share all of this with Detective Wilson. Make sure to tell him your author group knew when and where you were meeting with Jon Luis," Carlita said. "I wonder if Gina and the kids are up. I was thinkin' about taking the kids to Morrell Park and Leopold's for ice cream since it's not gonna rain today."

Mercedes phone chirped and she flipped it over. "It's the number for the police department, the station where Zachary works."

"It's either him or Detective Wilson," Carlita said. "You better answer it."

Mercedes nodded. "Hello?"

"Yes, this is Mercedes Garlucci. Yes, Detective Wilson. I was going to call you…you do? He did?"

Carlita leaned closer, eager to hear what the detective was saying.

Mercedes' eyes widened. "I told you last night. I never met Mr. Luis in my life. I have no idea why he had my address scribbled on a pad of paper inside his home."

Chapter 4

"Maybe he was checkin' you out before he met with you," Tony said in a loud whisper.

"Tell him about the other authors in your group," Carlita added.

Mercedes nodded. "Well, I was gonna call you anyways. I wanted to tell you I meet weekly with a group of other authors and we've been discussin' Jon Luis. They all knew about our meetin'."

"I see. Okay. Yeah. I'm not leavin' town." Mercedes told the detective good-bye. "Jon Luis died of a single gunshot wound to the back of the head. It doesn't sound like Detective Wilson is gonna look into questioning any of the authors in the group, but he is gonna question Autumn since she was packing heat last night. I think his plan is to try to pin Jon Luis' death on me or Autumn."

"I figured Autumn's gun was gonna get her in hot water one of these days." Carlita wiggled out of the chair and stood. "There's not much we can do about it this morning. I'm headin' downstairs to check on Paulie and the family. They should be out of bed by now."

Tony and Mercedes followed their mother into the apartment where Grayvie, Carlita's cat, gazed at them with mild interest. Carlita patted his head and scratched his ears. "Ever since I moved this table over by the door, Grayvie likes to sit on top and watch out the window."

Rambo waited until Carlita shut the door before bolting through the doggie door. "And this stinker refuses to use anything but his doggie door." She rubbed his back before giving a small treat to each of her pets. "I'll be back in a minute."

Carlita exited the apartment and made her way to Tony's apartment where she could hear the excited chatter of her grandchildren through the closed door. She rapped lightly and Paulie opened the door.

"Ma to the rescue. The kids are climbing the walls already," he groaned.

"Good. I thought I would take them to Morrell Park and then stop by Leopold's for some ice cream for breakfast."

"You're gonna let them eat ice cream for breakfast?" Paulie asked. "Don't let Gina find out. She'll have a cow."

Noel had joined her father at the door and her eyes grew wide. "Mommy is going to have a cow?"

"Daddy is being funny," Carlita said and then wagged her finger at her son. "That's what Nonnas do. They let their grandkids eat ice cream for breakfast." She pointed to the stairs. "Let's go get Aunt Mercedes."

Mercedes and Tony were waiting for Carlita and her grandchildren in the upper hallway.

"Are you coming with us, Uncle Tony?" Gracie asked as she slipped her hand in his.

"No Gracie. Uncle Tony has to work. Maybe you and Nonna can stop by later, on your way back." He gave his nieces and nephew a group hug.

"We'll bring you ice cream," Noel said solemnly.

Tony laughed. "But it will melt before you get it back here."

"I'll lick it on the way."

"I bet you would," Carlita said. "Maybe Uncle Tony can go with us next time." She turned to her son. "Don't forget to grab your key before you head out."

"I'm leavin' now," Tony said. "Got the keys here." He pulled them from his pocket and dangled them in her face before following the women and children downstairs. "Looks like it's gonna be a beautiful day."

"You're right," Carlita nodded. "I think we should go to the park first."

Morrell Park was bustling with dog walkers, kite flyers and Frisbee throwers. "Who wants to take the ferry across the river to Hutchinson Island?"

"Me," three small voices shouted in unison.

"This way." Carlita led them down the sidewalk, to the far end of the park and the *Savannah Belles Ferry,* which was getting ready to dock. They made their way to the back of the line.

"We're gonna go over there." Carlita pointed across the river, to the convention center and adjacent high-rise hotel.

Paulie hopped up and down on one foot. "Someday I'm going to be a captain and sail all over the world."

"I can't swim." Gracie moved closer to her grandmother.

"I hope we won't have to swim." Mercedes swooped down and picked up her niece. "We can sit on the lower deck, so you don't have to look at the water."

They waited for a handful of passengers to disembark before boarding the small ferryboat.

Gracie buried her face in her grandmother's arm as the ferry slipped away from the shoreline, but it didn't take long before she lifted her head and stared out at the water.

"See? It isn't so bad," Carlita said.

When they docked on Hutchinson Island, the group trekked up the ramp and steps to inspect the convention center. The center was locked and the parking lot empty, so they wandered around the hotel grounds, circling the meticulously landscaped gardens and large pool.

"Can we go swimming?" Noel asked.

"Not now," Carlita said. "Maybe later you can put your swimsuits on and I'll take you to the water fountains and splash park."

There wasn't much else to see, so they headed back to the dock and waited for the ferry to return. After boarding, they chose a bench seat on the side where they could look out the windows.

When they reached the other side, they wandered down the sidewalk, stopping to marvel at a large freighter that drifted past. They waved to a group of the ship's crew who were standing on an upper deck before making their way to the *Waving Girl* statue. After admiring the statue, the group retraced their steps out of the park.

"Let's get some ice cream," Carlita said.

The line at Leopold's was out the door and down the sidewalk. It took several minutes for them to reach the inside of the building and the order counter. Carlita ordered three child cones of chocolate chip, a single scoop caramel swirl for

Mercedes and a mint chocolate chip single scoop for herself.

Leopold's was packed and there wasn't an empty seat, so they maneuvered their way around the long line of people waiting to order to the sidewalk out front.

Mercedes adjusted her sunglasses and stared at the front of the building. "Let's walk to Oglethorpe Park. They have plenty of benches over there."

Carlita licked a circle around the rim of her cone and nodded. "And it's only a block away." She turned to her three grandchildren. "Hold on to your cones. We're not gonna go back for another one if you lose it."

She tightened her grip on her cone and placed her other hand on PJ's back. "Stay close to Nonna." The children obediently followed behind Carlita while Mercedes brought up the rear.

When they reached the park and an empty bench, Gracie held out her cone. "My cone is leaking."

Carlita pulled a napkin from her pocket and wrapped it around the cone. "That should help."

While they ate, Carlita and Mercedes discussed Jon Luis' death. "Are you gonna warn Autumn the detective mentioned questioning her?"

"I should text her." Mercedes single-handedly whipped her cell phone out of her back pocket, switched it on and began tapping the screen. "There. I sent her a message." The phone beeped before Mercedes had time to shove it back into her pocket.

"Too late." She squinted her eyes and studied the screen. "Detective Wilson already tracked her down, asking questions about her gun." She grew quiet. "It wasn't a match. The bullet that killed Jon Luis doesn't match Autumn's gun."

"That's a little good news," Carlita said.

"What if he thinks I shot Jon Luis and then tossed the gun into the river?"

"And then called the cops?" Carlita asked. "What killer would do that?"

They finished their ice cream and began to walk home, taking the long way around the block.

Mercedes slowed down when they reached *The Book Nook*. "Cricket is working." She waved to someone standing in the back of the store. "I want to tell Cricket what happened."

"Can we go in the bookstore Nonna?" PJ asked.

Mercedes reached for the door handle. "They have a children's section."

"Sure. I don't see why not," Carlita said.

The doorbell chimed as they stepped inside the cozy bookstore. A hint of mustiness, mingled with the scent of vanilla, lingered in the air.

"The books are over there," Noel said. Colorful, bright chairs, perfect for young children, surrounded low, round tables. Mini shelves lined the walls. A cardboard cutout of Paddington Bear peered down on the tables.

The children each grabbed a book from the shelves and settled in at the table.

"Hello Mercedes." A fiftyish woman with gray hair, pulled back in a tight bun gazed at them through gold round spectacles.

"Hi Cricket." Mercedes smiled. "My ma, nieces and nephew, and I just had breakfast ice cream at Leopold's. We were heading home and decided to stop."

Cricket grinned. "Ah. Breakfast ice cream. Can't go wrong with breakfast ice cream, especially if grandma suggests it." She winked at Carlita and Carlita immediately took a liking to the woman.

"I've been thinking about you this morning. How did your meeting with Jon Luis turn out?"

"That's another reason we stopped by. Jon Luis is dead."

Cricket clutched the strand of pearls hanging around her neck. "Oh dear."

Mercedes briefly told the woman what had transpired.

"And the police believe you're somehow involved in Mr. Luis' death?"

"It doesn't look good," Carlita spoke. "The fact that a young woman agreed to meet a complete stranger after dark in a secluded area is suspect."

"I wasn't alone," Mercedes reminded her mother.

"True. But it still doesn't look good." Neither mentioned to the woman that Autumn followed her to the meeting spot or the fact that the police found Mercedes' home address jotted on a pad of paper inside Jon Luis' home.

"You've lived in the Savannah area a long time," Mercedes said. "Is there anything you can recall seeing or hearing that involved Jon Luis?"

"Not right off the top of my head. Other than him working on several of Savannah's unsolved murders, including the Madison Square murder, which we've already talked about in our group." Cricket shook her head. "Such a shame. I guess Jon Luis carried his secrets to the grave."

"The people he was researching should be considered suspects," Carlita said.

"True," Cricket agreed. "Now that I think about the Madison Square murder, I believe all of the original suspects are dead." She clasped her hands together. "Yes, I'm certain they're all dead and several of them died under mysterious circumstances."

"They did?" Mercedes asked. Maybe they were onto something. "What if there's a serial killer out there, Jon Luis was nosing around and the killer decided to take him out?"

Carlita started to reply when PJ raced down the aisle to her side. "Nonna. This is my favorite book in the whole world. Can I have it?" He held up

One Fish, Two Fish by Dr. Seuss. Her granddaughters joined them, each carrying a book of their own. "Can we have a book, too?"

"Of course. Let's take them to the counter." Carlita followed Cricket and her daughter to the cash register.

Cricket rang up the purchases, swiped Carlita's debit card and handed it back before turning to Mercedes. "Will you be here for our author meeting this Thursday?"

"I hope so, unless I'm in jail."

"Bite your tongue," Carlita said.

"Here are your books." Cricket handed the children the books and smiled at Carlita. "It was nice to meet you."

"Same here," Carlita replied.

"I'll see you Thursday." Mercedes waved to Cricket, and then followed her mother and the children to the front of the store.

"I like this store," Noel said.

"Me too," PJ chimed in.

The group stepped back onto the sidewalk and continued walking home.

"You need to find out more about the murder she mentioned and maybe even do a little digging around in this Cricket woman's background," Carlita said. "She seems to know an awful lot about Jon Luis and the old murder case. What was it again?"

"It was called the Madison Square murder. It happened back in 1976. One of the original founding families, Teresa Honeycutt, was hosting a dinner party at their swanky home over in Madison Square. At some point during the party, a guest discovered Herbert Honeycutt's body. He'd been suffocated and his body stuffed in the dumbwaiter. Authorities arrested Teresa, his wife, but the charges were eventually dropped and the case was never solved."

When they reached the corner, they turned left toward home. "My guess is the wife did it," Carlita said.

"Teresa Honeycutt was a paraplegic. There's no way she could've strangled her husband and stuffed his body in the dumbwaiter. Most of the people at the party claimed they never saw or heard anything suspicious during the party. It was almost as if they were trying to cover up the murder."

Carlita mulled over Mercedes' words. Someone somewhere knew something about the Madison Square murder and Carlita knew exactly who that someone was.

Chapter 5

Victoria "Tori" Montgomery stepped into the library to join her unexpected guest. "It's so nice to see you Carlita. I've been meaning to stop by your pawnshop, but have been under the weather lately." She sniffed loudly. "Dreadful allergies this time of the year."

A uniformed servant glided in behind Tori Montgomery, carrying a silver tea set. "Bring the tray over here, Iris." She motioned to an antique table, situated between two powder blue French provincial chairs.

"Would you care for a cup of tea?" Tori turned to Carlita.

"Yes. Thank you." Carlita glanced outdoors, past the flagstone courtyard and the sparkling blue swimming pool. "There's something different about your pool."

"You're very observant. With the windfall of gems given to me by a dear friend, I decided to splurge and added a pool cabana with a half bath and a large changing room."

"Nice."

Iris handed Carlita a cup of tea. "Thank you, Iris."

The young woman nodded her head. "Will there be anything else?"

"No. That will be all for now." Tori waited until Iris exited the library and closed the door behind her. "I've always wanted a pool boy and this gives me the perfect excuse to hire one. Such a pity that I'll have to wait until spring to enjoy the new scenery."

Carlita coughed and covered her mouth to hide her smile. "You don't say."

"At my age, admiring from afar is one of life's little pleasures." Tori smiled and then her expression sobered. "When you called to ask if we could meet, I sensed you wanted to discuss something serious."

"Yes." Carlita sipped the tea and carefully placed the teacup on top of the fragile saucer. "Have you ever heard of the Madison Square murder?"

Tori shifted in her chair, eyeing Carlita over the rim of her cup. "Of course. Anyone who lived in Savannah during the mid-1970s has heard of the Madison Square murder. Does this have anything to do with Jon Luis' death over by the Riverfront District?"

"It does." Carlita explained Mercedes' involvement with Jon Luis and ended with Detective Wilson's questioning. "I think they're gonna try and pin it on my daughter. There's a killer lurking in Savannah and I believe Mercedes has been setup."

"Oh dear. Teresa Honeycutt died years ago, as well as all of the original suspects," Tori said. "The Honeycutt children moved away and I thought the whole sordid affair was long forgotten."

"Except for Jon Luis' investigation into the matter. Apparently someone wanted to silence him." Carlita folded her hands in her lap. "I'm afraid Mercedes, and perhaps even someone in her author group, could be next. I thought you might be able to shed some light on the whole matter and possibly point us in the right direction."

"The Honeycutt family and I ran in different circles, so I don't have much more information than what is available on the internet, although I always believed the investigators missed some important clues at the Honeycutt Manor, the scene of the crime."

Carlita perked up. "Really?"

"Yes." Tori nodded. "I, as well as many others in Savannah, believed someone…shall we say…greased the palms of the authorities, so they would drop the case."

"We call it sweepin' it under the rug. Too bad Mercedes and I can't take a look at the Honeycutt place."

"Perhaps you can," Tori said. "The place has changed hands numerous times over the years. The owners never stayed long, claiming the place was haunted."

"Haunted?"

"Aren't most old homes in Savannah rumored to be haunted? An entrepreneurial individual moved into the property a few years back and opened a restaurant. From what I've been told, they also offer ghost tours by appointment only."

"I'm surprised Mercedes didn't mention it to me." Carlita knew Mercedes would be all over that.

"They don't advertise, at least not that I've ever noticed," Tori said. "It's more a word of mouth about the ghost tours. Your best bet is to start asking around about the 1976 Tour."

"I will. Thanks for the info." The conversation shifted to Pirate Pete, the beautiful fall weather and Carlita's pawnshop business.

When Iris returned to check on them, Carlita glanced at her watch. "It's getting late. I should get going." She stood. "Give me a call the next time you're heading into town and maybe we can run over to the City Market for lunch."

"It sounds lovely." Tori accompanied Carlita to the front door. "I've been tossing around the idea of holding a fall ball Thanksgiving weekend. I haven't had one in years, and thought it might be time to shed my reputation as a recluse."

"A fall ball? It sounds intriguing," Carlita said.

"It is - or was - a grand affair, a chance to dress up. Guests disguise themselves with masks and there's a big reveal at the end of the party."

"I haven't been to a party in years."

"Neither have I." Tori opened the front door. "The more I think about it, the more I'm warming to the idea. It would be fun."

"Count me in." Carlita thanked Tori for the tea and the information and then headed to her car.

When she reached the road, Carlita rolled her window down and turned her radio up. Traffic on the main road, connecting Tybee Island to the mainland, was light and she hummed along with a catchy tune, enjoying the warm sea breezes as she drove.

Despite the cloud of suspicion hanging over Mercedes' head, things were going well. Carlita was looking forward to Thanksgiving and now Tori's party. It would give her an opportunity to meet more locals and perhaps even make some new friends.

When she reached the apartment building, she drove into the alley and parked in an empty spot next to Elvira. Carlita hadn't seen much of her troublesome tenant since her kidnapping at Fort

Pulaski, and it was almost a relief not to have to deal with the woman.

Carlita had stopped by Elvira's apartment the other day, after hearing a loud pounding sound coming from her place early in the morning. Elvira opened the door but refused to allow Carlita inside, telling her the apartment was a mess and she wasn't up to having guests.

Carlita peeked inside Elvira's car before wandering down the alley and into the apartment building.

Mercedes' Segway was gone and she remembered her daughter mentioning she had a lunch date with Detective Zachary Jackson. She confided in her mother she wanted to hear what he had to say about Jon Luis' murder investigation.

Carlita started to head up the steps, but changed her mind and made her way into the back of the pawnshop to see if Tony needed anything.

The store was busy and she caught her son's eye. He motioned for her to wait, so Carlita walked the aisles, straightening merchandise and checking out the new inventory of items.

When Tony wasn't working, he spent most of his free time with Shelby and Violet. The couple had planned to visit an art show in Charleston, South Carolina and were going to spend the weekend, leaving Violet with Carlita for a couple of days, but Shelby abruptly cancelled the trip, telling Tony she wasn't ready to leave Violet home.

Carlita didn't press the issue and hoped it wasn't because she didn't trust her to watch the young child. Or maybe when she found out Gina and her grandkids were coming for a visit, she didn't want to burden Carlita.

Although that wouldn't have been the case. Carlita loved Violet as if she were one of her grandchildren.

"Can I get some help over here?" A woman motioned to the jewelry display case, so Carlita grabbed the keys from the desk and made her way over.

"My grandmother had a cameo brooch almost identical to this." The woman pointed to an antique 14k white gold brooch.

"It's a gorgeous piece." Carlita lifted the brooch from the tray and handed it to the woman. "We had a pair of matching earrings, but it looks like we sold 'em already."

The customer turned the brooch over in her hand and squinted her eyes as she studied the price. "I see you're asking $275 for this piece. Would you be willing to take $175 cash?"

Carlita shook her head. "Unfortunately, I would lose money sellin' it to you for that low of a price. I'd be willing to go down to $250."

"$245," the woman countered.

"Sold," Carlita said. "You can pay over there."

The woman handed the brooch back, and they walked over to the cash register where Carlita rang up the purchase, wrapped the jewelry in tissue paper and slipped it into a plastic bag.

Tony made his way over and watched as the woman exited the store. "Look at Ma...wheelin' and dealin'. How much did she get you to come down?"

"The tag said $275 and I sold it for $245," Carlita said. "I hope that's okay."

"Not bad." Tony shrugged. "She's a regular. Comes by here about once a week, always lookin' for a bargain. I think she's got one of those online shopping sites for antiques. She buys from us, marks up the price and sells all over the country."

"Not a bad gig," Carlita said. "Maybe we should consider ramping up our own website and sellin' stuff online."

"It's a lotta work and I don't have time," Tony pointed out. "Plus, we have a decent spin on our merchandise as it is. If it ain't broke, don't fix it."

Carlita patted her son's arm. "As usual, you're right. It was just an idea. How you holdin' up with Paulie taking a few days off?"

"It's been a little hectic." Tony lowered his voice. "I heard him and Gina gettin' into it out in the hallway this morning. She was givin' him grief about the internet café business and..."

Tony's voice trailed off.

"And what?"

"Well, I wasn't gonna say nothin', but she said she wasn't gonna move here ever, so I think you can forget about that one."

Carlita frowned. "I'm not surprised. I shoulda known it wasn't gonna happen." She looked around. "Where's Mercedes? She said she was gonna help out today."

"She was in here earlier. She said she had some errands to run and that she'd be back right after lunch."

"I forgot she had a lunch date." Carlita whacked the palm of her hand to her forehead. "Duh."

The front doorbell chimed and Carlita watched as Detective Wilson stepped inside the store. He strode to the back. "Hello Mrs. Garlucci."

"Hello Detective Wilson."

"Looks like you got a nice operation going here."

"My son, Tony, has done an excellent job."

"I see." Detective Wilson cleared his throat. "This isn't a social visit. I'm here to take a look at the guns you have on hand."

Chapter 6

"You can't be serious." Carlita said the first thing that popped into her head. "My daughter didn't kill this Luis fellow."

"Mrs. Garlucci, I need to follow up on all leads. Your daughter was at the scene of the crime. She admitted she arranged to meet a stranger, after dark, in an out-of-the-way location and Mr. Luis made a point of checking your daughter out. Something isn't adding up."

"My daughter writes Maf...er, crime novels. She was doing research. Mr. Luis was investigating high profile, unsolved murders. My thinkin' is that someone out there didn't want Mr. Luis' investigations to see the light of day."

"There's always that possibility, but in the meantime I would like to check out your gun collection."

"They're over here." Tony led the detective to the gun case.

Detective Wilson removed several guns from the case and studied each one before jotting notes in a notepad. He slipped his notepad into his pocket, pulled out his cell phone and snapped several pictures of the guns. "Do you have any other guns here?"

"A couple, to protect the business." Tony led him to the office desk and showed him the guns.

After Detective Wilson inspected the guns, he headed toward the exit and Carlita hurried after him. "You didn't find a match, did you?"

"I can't discuss the case," the detective said as he reached for the doorknob. "I can appreciate your daughter's enthusiasm, and I admire anyone who can put pen to paper and come up with a story that doesn't come out sounding like a jumbled mess. In fact, I would love to write a book. Boy, have I got some stories to tell."

"I bet you do," Carlita murmured.

"Sometimes it's best to let sleeping dogs lie, if you catch my drift." The detective made his way out of the store. He shoved his hands in his pockets and casually strolled past the front window.

Carlita retraced her steps and watched as Tony carefully placed the guns back in the case and locked it. "What's your take?"

Tony shrugged. "I don't think he found anything."

The back door to the store flew open and Mercedes darted inside. "I think I mighta opened up a can of worms with this Madison Square murder investigation." She tugged her helmet off and fluffed her hair. "Zachary, I mean Detective Jackson admitted that after I told him about Jon Luis' death and my research into the murder, he decided to do a little digging around in the police department's records."

"And?" Carlita prompted.

"The Madison Square murder investigation records are sealed."

"Sealed as in no one gets to look at 'em?" Tony asked.

"Exactly," Mercedes nodded. "He said he's never seen anything like it before. Zachary is kind of a history buff. He likes to go through old cases when he's working desk duty and he said this was the first time he's ever run across sealed records."

Carlita leaned her elbows on the top of the gun display case. "Well, Detective Wilson was just here. He wanted to check out our guns for sale, probably because he's tryin' to pin this Luis' death on you."

"Great." Mercedes wrinkled her nose. "Did he find a match?"

"I dunno, but before he left, he said maybe you should let sleeping dogs lie. In other words, stop digging around in the old murder investigation."

"That makes it even more intriguing," Mercedes said. "Zachary told me the Honeycutt property is a restaurant, which I already knew, based on my research. What I didn't know is the owner offers tours. It's by invitation only."

"I heard the same from Tori Montgomery," Carlita said.

"Oh, I almost forgot you met with her. Was Ms. Montgomery able to shed any light on the Madison Square murder?"

"Not much," Carlita said. "Tori told me she didn't know the Honeycutts. They ran in different circles. She did say she thought the police ended the investigation prematurely and she suspects someone greased the palms of officials to close the case quickly."

"There's one more thing Zachary told me in confidence," Mercedes said.

"Oh?" Carlita lifted a brow.

"That Jon Luis recently filed a police report. His apartment was broken into and ransacked just over a week ago. From what he could see on the report, nothing had been stolen, but someone tore the place up." Mercedes glanced at the wall clock. "The author group and I are having a special get together at *The Book Nook* this afternoon to discuss Luis' death. I thought maybe we could contact the owner of the Honeycutt place and see if we can snag a tour."

"We, as in you and me?" Carlita asked.

"Yeah. I mean, unless you're scared it's haunted."

"I'm not scared," Carlita said. "If I was, I woulda moved out of this place a long time ago." Carlita's home had once been a casket company and more than one local had told her they believed it was haunted. There was also the fact that they'd discovered a body hidden behind a basement wall. Many people claimed numerous homes in the Savannah historic district were haunted.

"Why don't you check with Autumn first? If she doesn't wanna go, I'll go with you," Carlita said. "In the meantime, I'm gonna check on Rambo. I'm sure he's itchin' to go out." She headed upstairs while Mercedes stayed behind to help her brother.

Gina and Paulie, with the kids in tow, arrived a short time later and Carlita fixed sandwiches while she listened to them talk about their morning sightseeing activities.

According to Gina, the children loved the trolley tour, begged for a horse and carriage ride and settled for a trip to the children's museum instead.

Carlita finished making the sandwiches and Paulie helped his mother carry the food to the table. "Gina and I was thinkin' about taking the riverboat dinner cruise if you wouldn't mind watchin' the kids."

"Of course not," Carlita said. "We can pop popcorn and watch movies."

"Can we spend the night?" Gracie asked.

"Sure, why not?" Carlita wasn't sure how Tony would feel about camping out with his nieces and nephews, but it was only for one night and if it helped Paulie and Gina move a step closer to repairing their relationship, it would be well worth the minor inconvenience.

"A sleepover it is," Carlita said. "After you finish your lunch, you better run down to the pawnshop and warn Uncle Tony."

The children hurriedly finished their food and Paulie took them downstairs while Gina and Carlita cleared the table and washed dishes.

"I'm gonna run to the bathroom to freshen up," Carlita said, as she hung the dishrag on the edge of the sink.

"I'm gonna step outside for a sec." Gina made her way out onto the balcony where she reached into her purse and pulled out a pack of cigarettes.

Carlita's heart sank as she watched her daughter-in-law light a cigarette. The last time she'd seen Gina smoke was years ago, before the children were born.

She wandered into the bathroom and returned to the living room a short time later where she spotted Gina peering through the glass. When she caught a glimpse of Carlita, she began waving her arms.

Carlita walked over to the door and twisted the knob. The door was locked. "That's weird." She flipped the deadbolt and pulled the door open.

"I got locked out."

"I wonder how that happened." Carlita studied the deadbolt, flipping it back and forth. "It's a new door. We useta have a slider, but switched to French doors so I could add a doggie door for Rambo. We'll have to keep an eye on it, I guess."

"I'm gonna grab the kids and head to the apartment to put them down for a nap before tonight," Gina said. "I don't want them to be cranky when they get here later."

Carlita followed Gina into the hall. "I appreciate that, Gina."

"Thanks for offering to watch them."

Whack. Whack. The hall floor shook as the whacking noise, which was coming from Elvira's apartment, grew louder.

"What in the world is she doing in her apartment?" Carlita asked.

"You got your hands full with that one." Gina rolled her eyes and descended the stairs while Carlita strode to her tenant's door. She rapped loudly and when she didn't answer, she jabbed the doorbell. "Elvira! It's me. I know you're in there."

She tilted her head as she listened for footsteps, but there was nothing. "Elvira!"

There was still no answer and Carlita stomped back to her apartment.

"What was all that racket?" Mercedes hurried into the living room. "It sounded like a wrecking ball hitting the side of the building."

"Elvira."

"She's at it again. Did you knock on her door?"

"Yes. I rang the bell, too, and she didn't answer," Carlita said. "She's up to something. The fact she refused to open the door worries me."

"She's a trip," Mercedes said. "I hope she tones it down. I'm trying to write."

"I'm taking Rambo for a walk." Carlita slipped the leash off the hook and reached for Rambo's collar. "I bet you're gonna love having the kids over later, huh?" She clipped the leash to Rambo's collar and they headed outside. "Let's go to Walton Square."

As they walked, Carlita mulled over Luis' death and the comments Detectives Wilson and Zachary

Jackson had made. Was Mercedes playing with fire? Perhaps someone out there was desperate to keep the Madison Square murder buried.

Or maybe Jon Luis had other enemies. She made a mental note to talk with Mercedes, before she met with the other authors.

Rambo and Carlita circled the square and then strolled the center sidewalk, stopping to investigate several of the large oak trees before returning home.

When they reached the apartment, she hung Rambo's leash on the hook and headed to Mercedes' bedroom. The door was locked, so she rapped lightly.

The door flew open and Carlita jumped back, clutching her chest. "I will never, ever get used to you doing that."

"Sorry Ma." Mercedes leaned her hip against the doorframe. "What's up?"

"I wanted to talk to you about your author meeting and Jon Luis. What's the deal on this old mystery? Obviously, you've done your research, you and your author group. I want you to tell me everything you know."

"I'm learning more by the minute. Follow me." Mercedes waved her mother inside her bedroom. "I've been doin' a little more digging around. Have a seat."

Carlita perched on the edge of Mercedes' office chair while Mercedes reached for the mouse. "Here's a picture of the house at the time of the party and Mr. Honeycutt's death. Mr. Honeycutt was an architect. He also owned a wrought iron factory."

Mercedes straightened her back. "Have you ever noticed all of the ornate wrought iron on these historic downtown homes? Chances are Mr. Honeycutt's company, Honeycutt Ornamental Designs, sold them the ironwork."

Mercedes went on to tell her mother that, at the time the Honeycutt Manor was constructed, it was the largest, costliest home ever built in Savannah. "The Honeycutts lived the charmed life. Teresa was involved in a bunch of different social circles including several humanitarian groups. The woman dabbled in horse farms and even showed horses until her accident."

"Accident?"

"Teresa was thrown from a horse and paralyzed."

"What a terrible tragedy," Carlita said.

"The Honeycutts sued the owner of the riding stable. It was a mess. Half of the Savannah residents took the Honeycutt's side while the rest sided with the stable owners." Mercedes glanced at her watch. "I better get goin'. Don't want to be late for my meeting."

Carlita followed her daughter to the door. "Be careful."

"I'm gonna be keepin' a close eye on the others in the group. It's too much of a coincidence they all knew I was meetin' Luis and next thing you know, the guy takes a bullet."

Carlita followed her daughter to the bottom of the stairs and held the door while Mercedes steered her Segway into the alley.

"Oh. I almost forgot to tell ya. I snagged us a VIP tour of the Honeycutt Manor tomorrow night at nine." Mercedes hopped onto the Segway. "All I had to do was tell them we lived in Walton Square and owned the old casket company's building."

"Great," Carlita muttered. "I can hardly wait."

Chapter 7

Mercedes eased her Segway to the side of the bike rack, looped the cable around an end bar and snapped the lock in place. She removed her helmet and then made her way inside the small bookstore.

The tantalizing aroma of freshly brewed coffee wafted in the air and Mercedes sniffed appreciatively. She liked to tease Cricket that she knew how to lure new customers to the store by offering free samples of her gourmet coffees and tea.

The murmur of soft voices echoed from the back and Mercedes zigzagged around the biography bookshelf, past the travel section until she reached the conference room where the small group of authors regularly met.

She caught Stephanie Rumsfield's eye and made her way over to an empty seat.

"I'm glad you could make it," Stephanie said. "We've been sitting here, trying to figure out how on earth you managed to get caught up in Jon Luis' murder investigation."

"I was lucky enough to be in the wrong place at the wrong time." Mercedes slumped into the seat and slid her helmet onto the table. "What a mess."

Cricket hurried into the room carrying a carafe of coffee in one hand and juggling a stack of cups in the other. "I saw Austin walk in. The only person we're waiting on is Tom Muldoon. He called a short time ago and said he might be a couple of minutes late."

Mercedes took the coffee cups from Cricket. "I wonder if they serve decent coffee in prison."

"That's not funny," Cricket gasped. "We've got to figure out what happened to poor Jon Luis and clear your name."

94

"At least they didn't show your mugshot on the news," Austin Crawford drawled as he stepped into the room. "If you were gonna take him out, you shouldn't have told us about the meeting."

"I did not take him out," Mercedes said. "He was already a goner when I got there." She caught a movement out in the front of the store. "Tom is here."

Cricket stuck her head into the hall. "You got the front under control Tillie?"

"Yes ma'am." Tillie waddled to the doorway. "Now y'all holler if you need anything."

"Will do." Cricket closed the door as Tom Muldoon settled into an empty seat.

"Cricket said there was something to report on Jon Luis. Did you meet with him, Mercedes?" Tom asked.

"Sort of, except I didn't get to talk to him. When I got to our meeting spot, I found him lying on the ground, dead. He died of a single gunshot wound."

"How terrible," Stephanie said. "Maybe he was caught up in a love triangle and his lover shot him."

"Only a romance writer would come up with that conclusion," Austin said. "Or maybe it was one of those Hatfield and McCoys-type family feuds that spilled over from decades ago and an old enemy murdered him."

"Only a historical mystery writer would think that," Stephanie shot back.

"Touché'," Austin grinned.

"Regardless of the circumstances, the lead investigator, Skip Wilson, is determined to pin it on me," Mercedes said. "He stopped by our pawnshop earlier to take a look at our guns for sale and asked a bunch of questions."

"You're a mystery writer, Mercedes. What do you think happened?" Cricket asked.

"I don't know what to think, other than I'm still in shock. I have a couple pictures of the crime scene."

"Let's see," Tom said.

Mercedes whipped her cell phone out of her back pocket. "They're here somewhere. Ah, here they are." She handed her phone to Cricket, who slipped her reading glasses on and studied the pictures.

"He's in an unnatural position." She flipped to the second photo. "Are these his keys? Yes, I suppose they probably are. I see a pool of blood," she said as she handed the phone to Austin.

"Nothing noteworthy on the body, but the set of keys might be a clue," Austin said before passing the phone to Stephanie.

"Maybe Jon Luis was going to meet his lover and they're hotel room keys," she said.

"Let me look." Tom Muldoon quietly studied the photos. "I see a key fob. Luis probably locked his car door, turned around and met his murderer. Never even had time to put his keys in his pocket." He handed the phone to Mercedes.

"There's something else," Mercedes said. "The detective told me Luis had written my name down on a yellow pad. They found it in his apartment on his desk. I guess he was checkin' me out."

"Or maybe he wanted to check out what kind of books you already published," Cricket theorized.

"True. I hadn't considered that angle." The group discussed Luis' death at length. With little information to go on, they were unable to come up with any theories.

Mercedes almost told them about the 1976 Tour of the Honeycutt Manor, but decided against it. The other writers were also suspects, at least in her mind, and she didn't want to tip her hand that she planned to visit the scene of the Madison Square murder.

The conversation finally drifted to their current book progress. Stephanie was nearing the completion of her fourth romance novel in the *Savannah Sweet Romance Series.*

"You're a writing machine," Mercedes joked. "I'll be lucky if I finish my second novel by the end of January. Although, if I'm locked up in a prison cell, I'll have plenty of time to write."

"We won't let it happen," Cricket said.

Tillie rapped on the door, opened it a crack and peered inside. "Sorry Cricket. Got a customer out here who wants a refund."

"You can do a refund," Cricket said.

"He's returning a whole series."

"Fudge." Cricket slid her chair back and stood. "Are we still on for our regular meeting this week?"

"If I'm not in jail," Mercedes said.

"We're going to make you start paying each of us ten bucks every time you say that," Stephanie teased. She squeezed Mercedes' arm. "Don't worry. They got nothin' on you. After all, you have no family background that would cause the police to suspect you."

If they only knew!

The four of them stopped by the front desk to thank Cricket for the coffee and conversation before making their way out of the store. Tom climbed into his car while Stephanie headed toward the Riverfront District.

Austin wandered over as Mercedes slid her helmet on and snapped the clasp. "You want to head down to the Thirsty Crow one night to listen to your buddy, Cool Bones and his band play?"

"Sure," Mercedes smiled. "That would be fun and he would get a kick out of it."

"How about Friday night? I could swing by around seven to pick you up."

"It's a date...er, I mean a non-date," Mercedes said.

"Would it be such a terrible thing if it was a date?"

Mercedes felt her cheeks warm. "N-no," she stuttered. "It wouldn't."

She hurriedly told him good-bye and then hopped on her Segway before zipping off down the street. Mercedes was almost home when she realized she'd left her notepad and a portion of her new book draft on the conference table, so she did a quick U-turn and headed back to the store.

She stopped in front of the window, not bothering to lock her Segway since she planned to pop in, grab her stuff and head back out.

Mercedes stopped in her tracks when she looked inside the front storeroom window and spotted Tom, Austin, Stephanie and Cricket off to the side, huddled close together.

Chapter 8

Mercedes quickly backed up until she was out of sight and tilted her head as she watched the others in her author group. Stephanie was waving her hands frantically, while Cricket's arms were crossed, a serious expression on her face. Austin's expression was unreadable and Tom Muldoon was shaking his head.

She was almost 100% certain the group was discussing her. Why else would they be standing there? She'd watched Tom climb into his car as Stephanie walked away. A thread of suspicion crept into her mind. *Had she been setup? Were the other authors conspiring against her?*

They acted as if they wanted to help clear her name. She had never even heard of Jon Luis before someone in the group mentioned his name.

Mercedes turned her Segway around and tilted the handle forward as she sped home. When she reached the apartment building, she steered into the hall, yanked her helmet off and hung it on the handlebar before racing up the stairs, taking them two at a time.

Carlita and Gina were inside, sitting in the living room.

"Ma, you got a minute? I need to run somethin' by you."

"Sure." Carlita slid off the sofa. "I'll be right back."

"Take your time," Gina said. "I'll be out on the balcony."

Carlita followed her daughter to her room. "How did it go with your group of authors? Were you able to kind of feel 'em out, see what they thought of Luis' murder?"

"The meeting was great. Everyone was sayin' that they wanted to help me clear my name, but they were just flappin' their gums. Something is up." Mercedes went on to tell her mother the group exited the bookstore. She watched two of them leave while Austin hung back and asked her if she wanted to go out Friday night.

"Ah, another date?" Carlita lifted an eyebrow. "What about Detective Jackson?"

"It's nothin' serious. Neither one, at least not on my end." Mercedes waved her hand. "Well, I got flustered; I forgot the draft notes for my new book. I remembered when I was almost home, so I turned around and went back to get them. You never know when someone might be tryin' to steal ideas. I'm not sayin' my author friends would, but you never can be too careful."

"I agree. You have some great ideas, Mercedes."

"Thanks. When I got there, I stopped out front. That's when I noticed all of the other authors, Tom, Stephanie, Austin and Cricket, inside the store. They were huddled off to the side havin' a serious conversation."

"Maybe you left too soon," Carlita said.

"No. Tom was already in his car and Stephanie was halfway down the block when I left. I think they were waitin' for me to leave."

"What does this mean?"

"I don't know. It's a good thing I always keep a current copy of my book draft on the computer." Mercedes began to pace the floor. "What if they had a plan to set me up? They must think I'm dumber than a box of rocks. I gotta figure out if I was setup." She snapped her fingers. "I got it. I can tell them I can't make it to the next meeting. In the meantime, I'll ask Autumn if she would be willing to join the author group to spy on them."

"Do you think she'll do it?"

"There's only one way to find out." Mercedes pulled her cell phone from her back pocket. "I think she's workin' today. I want to ask her in person." Mercedes shifted her gaze. "Do you mind if she stops by later? I know you got all the kids coming over."

"Sure. The more, the merrier. Invite her for pizza," Carlita said.

"Thanks Ma." Mercedes had started to slip her phone into her pocket and it beeped. "She's fast. Yep. She said no prob-lemo." Mercedes shifted her gaze. "I didn't mean to interrupt you and Gina's chat."

"I think she was glad you interrupted. She's probably out on the deck smoking."

"Gina started smokin' again? I wonder what Paulie thinks."

"I dunno," Carlita said. "She's been sneakin' out onto the balcony while Paulie and the kids aren't around."

The women wandered out of the bedroom and made their way back to the empty living room.

Tap. Tap. Gina was out on the deck, tapping on the glass.

Carlita hurried across the room and unlocked the door. "You got locked out again?"

"Yeah." Gina stepped back inside; the lingering smell of cigarette smoke followed her in. "This time I heard it latch. I figured you'd be back in a minute, so no biggie. You better have it checked out before someone ends up stuck out there."

"I don't understand." Carlita flipped the lock back and forth. "We've never had a problem with it before. I'm sorry."

"It's okay." Gina glanced at her watch. "I'm sure the kids are up by now, and bouncing off the walls of the small apartment. If I was Tony, I'd go stir crazy in such a small space."

Carlita walked Gina to the door. "He doesn't spend a lot of time there. You still have to meet Shelby and Violet."

"Tony must really like her. I never heard him talk about a woman before." Gina shook her head. "Everything is Shelby this and Violet that. I wouldn't be surprised if he decides to step it up a notch."

"Propose?" Carlita asked.

"No. Shack up."

"Not on my watch," Carlita said. "If Tony wants to live with Shelby..."

"He's gonna have to put a ring on it," Mercedes joked.

"Exactly. You took the words right out of my mouth. He needs to put a ring on it."

"I'll be back in a coupla hours with the kids." Gina impulsively hugged Carlita. "Thanks for takin' the kids and for takin' Paulie in. I think the time he's spent down here has been good for him." She wagged her finger. "But don't be gettin' no ideas about us movin' down here."

"I had hoped you would consider it," Carlita confessed. "Of course, it would have to be you and Paulie's decision." She waited until Gina was downstairs before slowly closing the door behind her. "I guess that settles it."

"I think you should work on Vinnie instead," Mercedes said. "He's the one who still has both feet in the family business."

"True."

"I'm gonna log onto the computer to work on my book draft unless you need me for somethin' else."

"Nah. Bob Lowman sent a rough estimate for repairs to the restaurant. I haven't had a chance to go over it yet." Carlita settled in at the small desk while Mercedes returned to her room.

She worked on balancing her checkbook and then checked her email. Carlita's mind drifted to her husband, Vinnie, who had died in the early spring. There were times it seemed like yesterday and at other times, it seemed like eons ago. So much had happened since then.

During the days and weeks right after Vinnie first passed away, Carlita felt his presence, as if he was there with her all of the time, but now the feeling was starting to fade. Maybe it was because there were so many other things to occupy her mind and quiet moments were few and far between. Still, in those quiet moments, she could hear his deep voice and smell his cologne.

Carlita's eyes watered and she swallowed hard. In a way, Vinnie had helped her deal with his unexpected death when he made her promise to get their sons out of the "family business." Her promise kept her going, kept her moving, kept her pushing on.

That and the fact that she had something to prove to herself. When Vinnie was alive, she never had to worry about balancing a checkbook or budget for living expenses, let alone run a family business, which would soon be three family businesses.

She'd even learned how to drive, thanks to Mercedes mercilessly hounding her. Carlita had no idea what she would've done if her daughter hadn't been by her side. Mercedes' life had been almost as sheltered as Carlita's, but in their defense, it had been the only life they'd ever known.

The last thing she wanted to do was to have her daughter feel obligated to hang around and take care of her. No, Carlita was determined to prove to herself and her daughter that the Garlucci women could not only take care of themselves but also thrive, to enjoy life, to embrace new experiences.

Secretly, Carlita was thrilled Mercedes had started "non-dating" as she liked to call it, and how she had joined an author group on her own. Mercedes was starting to spread her wings, just like her mother.

A loud rap on the door pulled Carlita from her musings. "Must be Paulie and the kids." She hurried to the door and flung it open, coming face-to-face with Elvira, who was covered in a thick layer of gray dust.

"I'm glad you're home." Elvira shoved past Carlita and stepped into the living room. "There was a small fire in my back bedroom, but there's no reason to be alarmed. I put the fire out and am pretty sure I can patch the holes in the wall."

Chapter 9

Carlita's mouth fell open. "I knew it! I knew you were up to something."

"Hold your horses." Elvira held up a hand. "Like I said, I've got it all under control, but I figured I better head over here before you smelled smoke and called the fire department."

"What's going on?" Mercedes rushed into the living room.

"Elvira set her apartment on fire. I want to see the damage," Carlita gritted out. "You were already treading on thin ice."

"Don't be so dramatic." Elvira led the way out of the apartment and Mercedes and her mother followed. A thick cloud of smoke drifted into the hall and the heavy smell of smoke filled the air.

Beep. Beep. "Darn smoke alarms. I thought I unplugged them all," Elvira said. "I must've missed one." She darted inside the apartment, to the smoke alarm in the kitchen. She climbed onto the counter and teetered on the edge as she unscrewed the alarm and pulled out the battery.

The beeping stopped.

Carlita headed down the hall while Elvira hopped off the counter and ran after her.

"Don't freak out. It looks worse than it is."

"I'll be the judge of that."

Carlita stepped into a thick haze of smoke and her eyes started to burn.

Mercedes gasped, and said the first thing that popped into her head. "Elvira isn't worth going to prison over."

At first, Carlita had trouble wrapping her head around the mess, which centered on what appeared to be a bust. She stepped closer.

Despite the soot-covered nose and ear, the image was unmistakable. "Is this a bust of you?"

"Yeah. I was working on a self-image. I got bored with painting, so I switched over to table art, you know, the kind you display. I was almost done with it, too."

Elvira ran her fingertips over the charred hairline. "I thought it would be cool to add a bronze spy cap. It didn't turn out quite right and I read online where other artists used blow torches to smooth the edges."

"*A blow torch?* You used a blow torch inside your apartment?" Carlita yelled.

"The bust was too heavy for me to carry out to the courtyard," Elvira said in a small voice. She hurried on. "It would've been all right except the torch got a little too close to the curtains and they caught on fire. I ripped them down and was able to put out the fire, but I tore out a couple of small chunks of the drywall where the curtain rods screwed into the wall. I promise. I'll have this mess cleaned up in twenty-four hours."

Carlita closed her eyes and began counting. She opened her eyes. "You will clean this up and I'm starting the eviction process. This is the last straw." She turned on her heel and stomped out of the apartment.

"You can't throw me out on the street." Elvira ran after her. "I pay my rent on time. Well, I mean I pay my rent and right now, I'm current. It was a small mistake. I got so excited, I was careless."

Elvira followed her out of the apartment and to her front door. "Please. Give me another chance."

"I have been more than patient with you, Elvira. More than fair and even felt sorry for you, but this fiasco is beyond careless. It was downright dangerous. Fix the damage and start packing because you're out of here."

Mercedes slunk past her mother and into the apartment, thankful that she wasn't on the receiving end of Carlita's wrath.

She watched as her mother slammed the door in Elvira's face. "I can't say she didn't deserve that."

"I should've done it long ago," Carlita fumed. "I felt sorry for her. I can't let her continue her antics here. No wonder her previous landlord kicked her out."

Knock. Knock. "She doesn't give up!" Carlita jerked the front door open. "Now what?" she growled.

Paulie and Carlita's grandkids stood on the other side. "I. Are you okay Ma? You look like you're gonna punch someone in the face."

Carlita sucked in a breath. "I'm sorry Paulie. I just had a run-in with Elvira."

"Ah. I see," Paulie smiled. "It wouldn't happen to have anything to do with the smoke in the hall? I was gonna tell you, you need to check it out."

"I checked it out all right. Elvira tried to burn this place to the ground."

"You got it under control? Cuz I can run over there," Paulie said.

"It's under control."

"Okay. Uh. You sure it's a good time to leave the kids? Gina and I can do the dinner boat another time."

"No. I'm fine. Come on in." She ushered the children into the house. "Mercedes and I can handle it from here."

"Who's on your backpack?" Carlita forced Elvira from her mind and tapped the square yellow character on the front of PJ's backpack.

"Nonna, it's SpongeBob SquarePants," PJ said. "He lives in a pineapple at the bottom of the ocean."

"I wonder if he has room for Elvira," Carlita muttered as she turned to Noel. "And who is this on your backpack?"

"Elsa."

"I have Anna," Gracie said. "See?" She spun in a half circle, to show her grandmother the back of her backpack. "Can we make cookies? Mommy said we might make cookies."

"We are," Carlita nodded. "They're Great Nonna Garlucci's Italian Cookies."

PJ rubbed his tummy. "I'm starving."

"Let's have a snack, then we can start the cookies," Carlita said. "Later, we're gonna order pizza." She assembled three peanut butter and jelly sandwiches and then added celery sticks and ranch dressing on the side of each of the plates.

While the children ate, they told their grandmother about the places they'd visited. Carlita grinned as she heard all about Savannah through the children's eyes.

Mercedes breezed into the dining room. "You haven't started the cookies yet?"

"In a minute," Carlita replied.

"Can I help?"

"Of course. Why don't I supervise and you can help your nieces and nephew this time?"

The small kitchen wasn't large enough for three children, eager to bake and two adults, so Carlita sat in the dining room and watched as they mixed the ingredients and then each of the children took turns dropping cookie dough onto the greased cookie sheet.

While the cookies baked, they made the frosting. Carlita had slightly tweaked Great Nonna Garlucci's frosting recipe, by adding a small amount of cream cheese and lemon zest.

After the cookies finished baking and they waited for them to cool, the children and Carlita walked Rambo around the block, stopping by the pawnshop to find out if Tony would be around for pizza and cookies after the store closed.

"I'm goin' to Shelby's for dinner. I forgot to tell ya."

"If you change your mind, you can come on over. I'll order extra."

Tony promised he would and then Carlita and the children made their way back upstairs. After frosting and sampling their cookies, the children headed to the living room to watch cartoons while Carlita and Mercedes cleaned up the kitchen. "What time is Autumn coming by?"

"Around six o'clock. She's comin' right from work."

Carlita ordered a couple of pizzas along with some breadsticks for delivery and by the time the food arrived, Autumn followed the delivery driver inside.

"Ooh. You got Carmela's Pizza. I love Carmela's," Autumn smiled at the delivery guy. "Hey Zeke. I haven't seen you in a while."

The young man nodded. "I finally nailed a job as a customer service rep at the downtown IRS office. I'm staying on at Carmela's until the end of the week, so I can say good-bye to all of my regular customers."

Autumn wrinkled her nose. "We're gonna miss you down at the newspaper."

"I haven't seen you around there much either," Zeke said.

"I was promoted to assistant copy editor for digital services and my new cubicle is in the back of the building. They also upped my hours, so now I'm working full time."

"Congratulations. I thought you wanted to move into reporting."

"I do, but I'm gonna have to work my way up and I hope I do it fast. I hate reading and editing is the worst kind of torture," Autumn said.

"I better get a move on," Zeke said. "Nice to see you. Stop by the IRS office someday and say 'hi'."

Carlita collected the pizzas and handed Zeke a generous tip before passing the pizzas to her daughter. "He seems like a nice enough young man, and working his way up the ladder."

"He is, Mrs. G. We attended Savannah State University together, but never met until he started delivering pizzas." Autumn turned to Mercedes. "What's up? You sounded like you need a huge favor."

"I do," Mercedes said. "We can talk about it after we eat."

Carlita fixed pizza plates for PJ, Noel and Gracie, who sat at the table while the women headed to the living room.

Mercedes grabbed a slice of Hawaiian pizza and bit the end. "Are you working the day shift?"

"Yep. Got a raise, got a promotion, if you can call editing a promotion and I'm working full-time now."

"Does this mean you're not working say...Thursday evenings?" Mercedes asked.

Autumn shoved the rest of her first slice of pepperoni in her mouth and reached for a second slice. "Spill the beans. What do you want me to do on Thursday evening?"

"Join my author group over at *The Book Nook* and pretend you're a newbie author," Mercedes blurted out. "You only have to do it for a couple of weeks."

"It wouldn't be a lie. I've never written a single word in my life," Autumn said. "Why?"

"I think there's something going on in the group." Mercedes told Autumn how she'd met with the group and left, returning after forgetting something and then spotted the others in the group meeting without her.

"Maybe you just left before they did."

"Nope. Stephanie was already gone and Tom was in his car," Mercedes said. "I think they wanted to have a private meeting, when I wasn't around."

"Could be you're paranoid."

"So you're not going to help me out?" Mercedes asked.

"I didn't say I wasn't going to help. Of course I'll help, but you owe me one."

"A big one." Mercedes tore off a part of her breadstick and dipped it in the container of marinara sauce. "Carmela's does have pretty good pizza, but not as good as authentic New York style."

While they ate, Mercedes filled her friend in on the background of the other authors and offered some pointers on how to get a feel for what they thought of Mercedes.

"You're not gonna go to the meetings?" Carlita asked.

"No." Mercedes shook her head. "I'm gonna tell them I'm outta town, maybe that I had to head to New York."

After they finished eating, Autumn sampled the cookies before telling them she wanted to head home before dark. "Thanks for the pizza Mrs. G. Someday I'll make it to New York to sample the real deal."

"You're welcome," Carlita said. "Maybe you can go up there with us someday."

Mercedes walked Autumn to the bottom of the stairs. "Don't forget. The authors meet at *The Book Nook* this Thursday at six."

"Got it." Autumn gave a thumbs-up and hopped on her Segway. "Don't worry. If anyone can find out if the other authors are setting you up, it's me."

"Thanks Autumn." Mercedes watched as Autumn coasted to the center of the alley and then sped off, disappearing from sight.

Carlita kept her grandchildren busy, drawing pictures and arranging them on the refrigerator. After finishing their artwork, they started to watch a movie. Halfway through, she caught two of them dozing off, so she took turns getting them ready for bed.

Instead of having the children sleep in the living room where Tony would wake them up when he came home from Shelby's, she decided to let them sleep with her in her king size bed.

She'd forgotten how much young children flopped around and woke up several times during the night. One time, PJ's heel was pushing against the side of her forehead.

Gracie was the first to wake and she began to wiggle around, which woke the others.

Carlita left them in the bedroom to watch television while she toasted some pop tarts and carried them, along with some fruit, back to the bedroom in an attempt to let Tony and Mercedes sleep a little longer.

Despite her best efforts, the children began to giggle and run around the small room.

"I thought I heard someone giggling." Mercedes stuck her head in the room. "Were you the one giggling?" She swooped Gracie into her arms and began tickling her. "Yep, this is the giggler."

She set her on the floor and Gracie scampered off.

"Are you really gonna evict Elvira?" Mercedes asked.

"Don't tell me you stayed up all night worrying about Elvira."

"No. She was the least of my worries, but I heard some thumping out in the hallway already this morning. I figured it was her."

"She better be fixing the mess she made," Carlita said. "And, yes, I am going to evict her before she burns our home and business down to the ground."

The thought of Elvira made Carlita's blood boil. She'd reached her limit with the woman and there were ample sections of the lease Elvira had broken where it would be easy to get the woman out.

"Don't forget about our 1976 Tour tonight," Mercedes said.

"I already forgot. What time is it?"

"It starts at nine. I'm gonna do a little more research today, before we head out."

"Great," Carlita groaned. "I can hardly wait to track down ghosts."

Chapter 10

"Do you want me to go with you?" Mercedes pointed at the eviction papers in Carlita's hand.

"No. Thanks for the offer, but I can handle this. If I'm gonna be a business owner, I'm gonna have to get used to doin' unpleasant things," Carlita said. "Elvira knows this is coming. The sooner I get this over with, the better."

Carlita had almost changed her mind about evicting her pain in the rear tenant. Almost. But she had put up with enough. On the one hand, she believed that deep down Elvira hadn't set out to damage Carlita's property and it wasn't intentional when she impulsively placed herself in dangerous predicaments. It was the principle of the matter, and Elvira's antics seemed to be escalating. "I'll be back in a minute."

Carlita sucked in a deep breath, flung the door open and marched across the hall where she rapped loudly on her tenant's front door.

The door opened a crack.

"I'm here to serve you with your eviction notice," Carlita said.

The door opened. Elvira held out her hand. "Okay."

Carlita handed the papers to her. "That's it? You're not gonna raise a stink?"

"Nope." Elvira shrugged her shoulders. "I knew after the small incident with the fire that you were going to follow through with your threat. Plus, my six-month lease is up in a couple of months. I've been on the hunt for a new place. I need to live somewhere that's a little less rigid. All these rules and regulations are cramping my style."

"No hard feelings?" Carlita asked.

"Not at all," Elvira said. "I'll have this place fixed up and looking brand new by the end of next week. In the meantime, I plan to start moving my stuff. I've already signed the paperwork for my new place and I have the keys."

She shifted to the side and pointed to a moving box on the floor near the door. "I'm clearing out the damaged bedroom first, so I can work on it." Elvira placed the eviction papers on her desk. "I will get my deposit back and pro-rated rent that I've already paid, right?"

"Technically, you signed a six month lease." Carlita paused. "I'll cut you a deal and let you out of your lease a little early, but you won't get a refund for the rest of this month and if the apartment is in move-in condition after you're out, I'll refund your deposit."

"That's gonna put me in a pinch," Elvira said. "Paying rent on two places."

Carlita lifted an eyebrow.

"Okay. It's a deal." Elvira picked up the box and followed Carlita into the hall. "Can you pull my door shut?"

Carlita pulled the door shut and followed Elvira to the top of the stairs. "You're gonna have to make a ton of trips moving your stuff in your little car."

"I'm not driving to the new place. I'm walking." Elvira shifted the box and slowly made her way down the steps. "Walton Square is a desirable location. It took some digging around to find a vacant space in this area, enough room for an apartment, a storefront to sell and display my artwork, not to mention a place where potential clients who are looking to hire EC Investigative Services can come."

"You're moving somewhere here in the neighborhood?" Carlita stumbled down the stairs and followed Elvira into the alley.

"Yep. I'm moving over there." Elvira nodded at the building on the other side of the alley. "Got it for a steal. The rent is even less than what I was paying you. It's a little rough around the edges, but with my track record it's probably better that way. You wanna check it out?"

"I thought it was for sale." Carlita hurried to keep up with Elvira.

"The owner, Davis, took it off the market. I'm renting it month-to-month, but figured if my investigative business or art store takes off, I might put in an offer myself."

The color drained from Carlita's face. "Y-you would be my permanent neighbor."

"Cool huh? Can you hold the box while I get the key?"

Carlita took the box and waited while Elvira fumbled inside her pocket and pulled out a single key. "I'll have to change the locks. It's on my to-do list, right after I fix the teensy amount of damage to your apartment."

"It's not teensy. There's extensive smoke damage not to mention holes in the wall."

"An easy fix." Elvira twisted the key and pushed the door. It groaned loudly in protest. "I still have to get the power turned on. I left a flashlight over here."

Carlita caught a whiff of a musty smell and followed Elvira into the large, open space.

"It's like a blank canvas." Elvira switched the flashlight on, illuminating the cavernous interior of the main floor. "I figure I can add a wall over there and put EC Investigative Services on that side. I won't need much space, only enough room for a desk, a couple of chairs and a waiting area."

She made a sweeping motion with her hand. "The art showroom will take up more space. I plan to bring in other artists to rent out sections and if I play my cards right, I'll be living here rent-free." She stepped over to a dilapidated counter, which sported a chipped, cast iron sink. "It's got the basics, although it could use a little deep cleaning."

"Or a gut job," Carlita muttered.

Elvira ignored the comment. "The bathroom is over here." She tugged on a small door. "It's a little cramped. Since it's only me, it'll work for now."

"I can appreciate your optimism, Elvira, but this place needs a lot of work." Carlita stepped into the small bathroom and bounced on her tiptoes as she peered out the grimy window in front of the sink. It was eye level with Carlita's rear entrance.

She shifted her gaze to the second story. There was an unobstructed view of Carlita's balcony.

"Great view of your place, huh? I'll show you the rest."

Carlita exited the small bathroom and followed Elvira across the open space to the front. She opened the door and they stepped out onto the sidewalk. "This place has excellent street exposure. I figure one of those custom flashing signs should get potential customers attention."

"What about parking?" After Elvira moved out, Carlita would need the empty parking spot for a new tenant.

"It's down here." The women made their way to the end of the block and turned left. Elvira stopped abruptly in front of two large gray gates. "I don't have a key yet, but you can see a double parking spot back here." She tilted her head and eyed Carlita. "I could rent out one of the spaces to you for extra tenant parking."

"That's a thought."

"I heard about Mercedes' mess and the author's death down by the river." Elvira shook her head. "I wish I could help dig into it a little, to see if I can find anything out, but I have my hands full."

"I appreciate the offer," Carlita said. "I'm hoping the investigators will be able to track down

Jon Luis' killer instead of trying to pin it on my daughter."

The women retraced their steps and Carlita stopped when she spotted a rusty wrought iron gate. "You have a courtyard?"

"Yeah. I forgot to mention it," Elvira kicked the bottom of the gate and it creaked as it swung open. "It needs some cleaning first, but I think it will be the perfect spot to work on my art."

Thick vines covered the brick walls. Carlita inched forward, keeping to the center of the overgrown walkway when she stumbled on a cobblestone that jutted out. Her arms flailed wildly as she fought to regain her balance.

"I forgot to mention you need to watch out."

The interior of the courtyard was in the same sad state of disrepair as the inside of Elvira's new home.

Carlita said the first thing that popped into her head. "You have your work cut out for you." They stepped into the center of the courtyard where Carlita spun in a slow circle. "There's plenty of space. I think it might even be a little larger than my courtyard once you get rid of the overgrown brush and weeds."

"Yep. But first things first." Elvira led the way as they wandered out of the courtyard. She pulled the gate shut. "I have to get my apartment in tip top shape. I'm gonna need my deposit money back, so I can start working on this place."

"It shouldn't take you long," Carlita said. "If, as you say, they're only minor repairs."

The women re-entered the building, strode across the open space and stepped through the back door, into the alley. While Elvira locked up, Carlita strolled to the center of the alley and studied the exterior of the building and the second story windows that faced her apartment.

Elvira joined her.

"What about the second story?" Carlita pointed up.

"I haven't been up there. The stairs are in the back, up the left side but there's a shiny new deadbolt on it." Elvira shrugged. "I tried to pick the lock but it's one of those heavy-duty ones. I'm tempted to shimmy up the side of the building one of these days to have a look around."

The women stepped back into the lower hall of their apartment building and Carlita closed the door behind them. "If you need help moving the big stuff over to the new place, holler and I'll have Paulie and Tony take it over there for you."

"Thanks Carlita. I might take you up on the offer." Elvira grabbed the handrail. "Dernice should be here any day. She can help me move whatever smaller stuff I have left. I'm sorry for any trouble I've caused you. I know I can be a little impulsive."

"A little?"

"Okay, a lot," Elvira said. "But I never meant any harm."

"Let's let bygones be bygones," Carlita patted Elvira's arm. "I'm glad you didn't burn my place down."

"Whew!" Elvira rolled her eyes. "Me too. For a minute there, I thought the place was a goner. As soon as I have the bedroom repaired, you can come over and check it out."

She sauntered across the hall to her door. "It's gonna be kinda lonely living over there by myself."

"Look at it this way, instead of being across the hall, you'll be across the alley," Carlita said, although she wasn't sure if that was going to be a good thing, or a bad thing.

Chapter 11

"Are you almost ready Ma?" Mercedes hollered into the hall. "We gotta get a move on or we'll be late for the ghost tour."

"I'm ready." Carlita ambled into the living room. "Are you sure I should be wearing all black?"

"I don't want to stand out," Mercedes said.

"And you don't think wearing all black will make us stand out?"

Mercedes ignored her mother's question and pointed at her dangling purple earrings. "I would ditch the earrings if I were you. I read somewhere that ghosts like to attach themselves to gemstones. We don't wanna be bringin' any unexpected guests home."

"Better safe than sorry." Carlita removed the earrings and set them on the table next to the door. "I'm ready."

"We're gonna have to hustle." The women hurried into the hall, down the stairs and out into the alley. "It's about a ten minute walk, which should get us there at nine on the dot." Mercedes patted her pocket. "I got the forty bucks to pay for the tour in my pocket."

"Cash?"

"Yeah. They only take cash," Mercedes said. "It's kinda weird. You gotta have connections for a tour invitation and then the confirmation comes from someone with the email username *looming darkness.*"

"What is the owner's name?" Carlita was beginning to dread this tour more by the minute.

"Don't freak out, but his name is TG Flinch."

"An owner with the name TG Flinch and an email with the username looming darkness. Now

143

why on earth would that make me nervous?"
Carlita asked sarcastically. "We'll be lucky if we
make it out of this tour alive. If they ask us to
leave our cell phones and belongings at the door,
I'm gonna turn around and walk right back out."

"You worry too much." Mercedes slowed.
"We're here."

Carlita squinted her eyes and peered over the
top of the spiked metal fence posts. She lifted her
gaze and stared at the steep steps and the blood
red columns guarding the front door. Two
lampposts stood sentinel near the base of the
steps and yellow flames licked at the sides of the
glass globes.

"Let's go, before you change your mind."
Mercedes grabbed her mother's arm and dragged
her through the gate and up the steps. She rapped
on the metal door knocker and a shadow passed
by the etched glass window pane before the door
opened.

"Yes?"

"I-uh, am Mercedes Garlucci. My ma and I are here for the 1976 Tour."

The door opened wide and the women stepped into the dark hallway. Flickering gas lanterns lined both sides of the walls, illuminating the red velvet wallpaper, which happened to be the same shade as the exterior columns.

Carlita turned to the person who had greeted them. It was a woman, and she was dressed in red from head to toe. "I see a theme here with the color red."

Mercedes pinched the back of her mother's arm.

"Ouch."

"Are you TG?"

"I am," the woman whispered. "You'll have to leave your belongings in the box." She drifted to an antique steamer chest and lifted the lid. "In here."

Carlita spun on her heel, preparing to bolt when Mercedes reached out and grabbed her mother's arm. "We can't leave now," she hissed under her breath.

"I'll wait for you out front," Carlita whispered in a loud voice. "If you don't come out in forty-five minutes, I'm callin' the cops."

"Is there a problem?"

Carlita could've sworn TG "floated" across the room and she was now certain the woman was an apparition.

"My ma doesn't want to leave her belongings behind." Mercedes forced a laugh. "Trust no one. It's one of the downfalls of livin' most of your life in New York City."

The woman slowly turned and faced Carlita. "You own the old Smythe place on Mulberry Street?"

"Yes, my husband, Vinnie, owned it. We moved down here after he passed away." Carlita grabbed the doorknob. "I'll be outside."

"You can keep your belongings with you," TG whispered.

"Great." Mercedes said. "Let's go."

Carlita stubbornly refused to budge.

"Ma. She said you could keep your purse. Let's start the tour," Mercedes urged.

Carlita reluctantly trailed behind her daughter and TG as they moved from the hallway to the parlor, through the dining room and then into the dated kitchen while TG shared with them a brief history of the home.

"I'm sure you're here to see the infamous dumbwaiter. It's over here." TG floated to the other side of the kitchen, lifted a skeletal arm and pointed a long red fingernail at a scuffed wooden cabinet door.

Carlita tiptoed over to the cabinet. "May I?"

"Yes." TG nodded. "Mr. Honeycutt is long gone."

"And only his spirit remains," Mercedes joked.

Carlita cautiously opened the cabinet door and Mercedes peered over her mother's shoulder at the interior of the tall, rectangular box.

"Mr. Honeycutt wasn't a tall man if he fit in here." Carlita leaned forward, stuck her head inside the dumbwaiter and gazed up. She glanced behind her at their tour guide. "I swear we got a few ghosts over at our place. You ever see ghosts here?"

"Yes. All the time." TG didn't elaborate. "Would you like to see the restaurant dining room and kitchen? They're both closed now."

"Sure." Mercedes peeked inside the dumbwaiter and then hurried to catch up with her mother and TG, who were already walking down a narrow hall to the back of the property.

TG pushed a swinging door open and they stepped into a light, bright, state-of-the-art, gleaming commercial kitchen.

Carlita blinked rapidly. "Wow. I never saw this one comin'."

Mercedes jostled in next to her mother. "Holy smokes."

"Do you mind if I take a picture of your kitchen? I'm gonna be openin' an Italian restaurant soon and I need some ideas."

"You're Italian?" TG asked and then chuckled at her own joke. "I'm kidding. Your accent is a dead giveaway, not to mention the Garlucci name."

Carlita snapped several pictures of the kitchen with her cell phone and then they followed TG into the restaurant's main dining room. It was an eclectic mix of nautical, nostalgia and musical. "What's the name of your restaurant?"

"The Ghost Roast. We serve mostly burgers, sandwiches and wings. Pub type food," TG said. "The name works nicely with my initials...TG, the ghost."

Now that they were in the bright light, TG didn't look nearly as "apparition-y." She appeared to be young, closer to Mercedes' age if Carlita had to guess.

"My real name is Tierney Grant, not as spooky and mysterious as TG Flinch."

"True," Mercedes agreed.

The trio chatted about the restaurant business and Tierney gave Carlita and Mercedes some tips, telling them if they needed any advice, she would be happy to help them.

Mercedes waved her hand around the room. "How did you happen to get into the restaurant and ghost tour business?"

Tierney smiled. "The same way you did. I inherited it."

"Before I forget." Mercedes reached into her pocket, pulled out two crisp twenty-dollar bills plus a ten and handed them to Tierney. "Thanks for the tour. I am a little disappointed we weren't able to learn more about the Madison Square murder and Mr. Honeycutt's death."

"I've tried to do a little digging around myself," Tierney said. "No one in Savannah wants to talk about it. It's a big mystery."

"And cover-up," Mercedes nodded. "I found out about Jon Luis from my author group. The man was working on a book about the Madison Square murder. We planned to meet but he died before I had the chance to talk to him."

Tierney's eyes widened. "I planned to meet with Mr. Luis, too. He disappeared off the face of the earth a few years back and then I started hearing rumors he was back in Savannah. Out of the blue, he called me and we began emailing back and forth."

Mercedes' heart skipped a beat. "You did? Did he say anything about the Madison Square murder?"

Tierney shook her head. "He said he would only discuss it in person and I think the reason he agreed to meet me was because he wanted to search this place. He claimed he was close to solving Mr. Honeycutt's murder, but needed to double check something."

"What a strange coincidence," Carlita murmured.

"I don't think it's a coincidence," Tierney said. "Your home, the Smythe place, was also the old George Delmario place. Jon Luis told me he was working on three unsolved murder cases in Savannah."

"His book was about Herbert Honeycutt, who was murdered here and George Delmario, who was murdered at our place? I wonder who else he was investigating," Mercedes mused.

"I wish I knew," Tierney said as she accompanied them to the front door. "I guess we'll never know if Jon Luis figured out who killed Honeycutt."

Carlita thanked Tierney for the information and they wandered out onto the sidewalk.

Mercedes waited until they were a safe distance from the house before speaking. "Do you think Tierney was lying and she met with Jon Luis?"

"I dunno, Mercedes. What we do know is your author group knew when and where you were meetin' Jon Luis. If Tierney is right, and Jon Luis was working on the unsolved cases, it would make sense he would agree to meet you. He was probably gonna cut a deal where he shared info on the case in exchange for access to our property."

Mercedes snapped her fingers. "It makes perfect sense and ties in with what Detective Wilson said, how Jon Luis had written my name and address on a piece of paper. He was already doin' research on George Delmario's death."

"Well, he wouldn't have gotten far, snooping around in Delmario's murder, before someone from the family up north got wind of it and came down here to tie up another loose end," Carlita said. "I have a hunch someone in your author group is either Jon Luis' killer or knows something about it."

"I'm getting the same feeling and I asked Autumn to attend the author group. I hope I didn't set her up to face a killer."

Chapter 12

Autumn tucked her cell phone under her chin as she spoke. "Don't worry. This'll be a piece of cake. My story is almost airtight. Even if the others become suspicious, they can check me out. I work at the newspaper and I'm working on my first novel."

"I hope you're right," Mercedes said uneasily. "I got a bad feelin' about all of this. The more I think about it, the more I'm certain someone in my group is linked to Jon Luis' death."

"Or this Tierney chick you met. She sounds suspicious to me. Didn't you say she inherited the Honeycutt property, but didn't elaborate?" Autumn pointed out. "I talked to one of my inside guys at the police department and he gave me some new info on Jon Luis' case."

"What did he say?"

"Listen, I gotta run or I'll be late for the meeting," Autumn said. "I'll stop by after it's over."

"Okay, be careful," Mercedes said.

"Will do." Autumn disconnected the line and shoved the phone in her back pocket. She stepped inside *The Book Nook* and made her way to the counter in the back. A plump woman standing behind the counter looked up, peering at her over the rim of her glasses. "Can I help you?"

"Yes. I'm Autumn Winter. I'm here to meet with Cricket Tidwell and some other authors."

"Welcome Autumn." The woman smiled widely. "The rest of the group is already here. They're in the conference room right over there." She pointed to an open door.

"Thank you." Autumn stepped across the hall and stuck her head inside the room.

An older woman sprang from her chair. "Autumn?"

"Yes," Autumn nodded. "I'm Autumn Winter."

"Welcome." The woman waved her into the room. "We're glad you're here."

"Thank you for allowing me to join your group, at least for tonight."

"We hope you find our group's input useful and decide to join us on a permanent basis. I'm Cricket Tidwell, owner of *The Book Nook*." The woman pointed to an empty chair. "If you'd like to have a seat, we'll go around the table, introduce ourselves and share a little about our writing."

Autumn eased into the empty seat and her heart sank when she noticed the others in the room each had a manila folder and yellow notepad in front of them. "Oh no. I just left work. I forgot my manuscript. I was in a hurry and didn't want to be late."

"It's okay, dear." Cricket patted her hand. "You can bring it next time, if there is a next time." She changed the subject. "I'll start with me. I've been writing under my pen name, Cricket Tidwell, for

157

over twenty years. I write non-fiction, mostly cook books, crocheting books and cat care. The three C's."

The woman at the other end of the table spoke. "I'm Stephanie Rumsfield. I'm the newbie of the group, if you don't count Mercedes, who isn't here tonight. I write romance books...think Harlequin and I've been writing since the early 90s. My boyfriend and I moved here from Montana earlier this year."

The man seated next to Stephanie cleared his throat. "Welcome Autumn. I'm Tom Muldoon. I've been writing thriller/suspense novels for years, although I don't write as often anymore. It's more of a hobby for me."

The young man next to Tom spoke. "Hi Autumn. I'm Austin Crawford and I write historical mysteries and recently started releasing books in a new Civil War era series."

"And Austin recently made it to the Publisher's Weekly bestseller list," Cricket said.

"Ah, so we have someone famous in our midst," Autumn joked.

"Why don't you tell us about yourself, what book you're working on and why you decided to become a writer," Cricket said.

Autumn's eyes widened. "I...uh. I work as a copy editor at the Savannah Evening News and, to be honest, my goal is to become a news anchor. I started dabbling in writing. It seemed like a natural fit..." Her voice trailed off.

Stephanie leaned back in her chair and crossed her arms. "What genre are you writing in?"

Autumn said the first thing that popped into her head. "Outer space fantasy. Romance."

"You mean like space opera romance?" Tom asked. "That's an interesting genre."

"It could also be considered sci-fi romance," Stephanie said. "It is interesting. What's the premise of your story? I'm intrigued."

"Two warring families escape an exploding planet earth and join forces on Zebulon to save their species from extinction," Autumn said. "I don't have my notes and I'm a little nervous. I can't remember the details."

"What's the name of the book?" Austin asked.

Autumn's mind raced as she tried to think of a name. "Zebulon Galaxy: The Final Frontier."

"Sounds like an old Star Trek movie," Tom said.

Autumn laughed nervously. "And I thought I made it up." Her armpits grew damp and she shifted in her chair.

"We're making Autumn nervous," Cricket said. "Sorry dear. We're excited to have you here since we're down one with Mercedes gone."

"Who is Mercedes?" Autumn asked.

"Mercedes Garlucci," Austin said. "She lives nearby and writes mafia mystery and suspense.

You would like her. She's about your age and has some great ideas."

"I'm sure I would," Autumn said. "Writing mob books would be interesting."

"We're not sure if she's coming back," Stephanie said. "She's being investigated."

"Stephanie," Austin said.

"What? It's not like it's a secret. If Autumn works at the newspaper, I'm sure she's heard all about it."

"Being investigated?" Autumn squeaked.

"She's under investigation after she found a man's body down by the river," Tom said. "It's not fair to talk about Mercedes when she's not here to defend herself."

"I agree," Austin said. "Let's discuss our work in progress."

Autumn attempted to appear interested in the other authors' books, but she was bored to tears and caught herself dozing off twice.

The second time it happened, Cricket called her out. "You seem very tired, Autumn. Are you feeling all right?"

"I took an allergy pill on my way here and they always make me sleepy," she yawned.

"It's getting late. I think that about wraps up our meeting for tonight." Cricket stood, a sign the meeting was over. "Do you think you'll join us again next week Autumn?"

"I'll try. I do appreciate the invitation. It's a little intimidating to see how far all of you are in your writing careers while I'm still working on the draft for my first book."

"We all had to start somewhere," Stephanie said. "You mentioned you were a copy editor at the Savannah Evening News. Are you ever in the market for part-time work? I could use a good copy editor."

"Me too," Austin said.

"Between work and trying to write, I don't have a lot of free time, but I can ask around to see if anyone who works in my department is interested in making a little extra money."

"That would be great," Stephanie said.

Autumn promised to put the word out and then hurried out of the bookstore. She strolled to the end of the block before turning left and making her way to *Shades of Ink*, her brother's tattoo parlor, where she'd parked her Segway. She popped in to tell him she was stopping by Mercedes' place before continuing toward the apartment.

After waiting for a horse and buggy tour to pass by, Autumn crossed the street and stepped into the alley behind the Garlucci's property.

Autumn caught a glimpse of a woman sitting on Mercedes' balcony and a whiff of cigarette smoke drifted down. She didn't recognize the woman and figured it must be Paulie's wife, Gina.

She gave the woman a small wave and jabbed her finger on the buzzer connected to Mercedes' unit when the door opened and Elvira Cobb emerged.

Autumn jumped out of the woman's way as Elvira eased a large box through the open doorway and stepped onto the stoop. "Do you need help?"

Elvira peered around the side of the box. "Nah. I'm just going across the alley."

Autumn watched as Elvira disappeared inside the building on the other side of the alley, stepped inside and then closed the door behind her.

Mercedes met her at the bottom of the stairs.

"What's up with Elvira?" Autumn asked. "She carried a box into the building across the alley."

"Ma kicked her out."

"For real?" Autumn blinked rapidly. "She must've done something over the top this time for Mrs. G to kick her out."

"She almost burned our building to the ground. We thought we were gonna get rid of her for good. Instead, Elvira rented the main floor of the building behind us."

"She's like a bad rash," Autumn laughed. "Are you gonna start looking for another tenant?"

"Maybe. I'm not sure. Ma is so fed up right now; she might let the apartment sit empty. C'mon in." Mercedes waved her friend up the stairs and inside the apartment.

Rap. Rap. A small commotion coming from the deck door caught the women's attention.

"It looks like Gina locked herself out on the balcony again." Mercedes hurried to the balcony door and flipped the lock. "You got locked out again?"

"It's your cat." Gina stepped inside the apartment and pointed at Grayvie, who was lounging on the small table next to the door. "I watched him jump up on this table and flip the lock."

"Grayvie has been locking you out?"

The cat flopped onto his side and yawned.

"I can't believe he locked the door."

"I think he's got it in for me. Watch this." Gina stepped onto the balcony and closed the door behind her.

Grayvie scrambled onto all fours and began swatting at the lock. *Click.*

After flipping the lock, he flopped back down on the table.

"That was cool," Autumn unlocked the door. "I mean, not cool for Gina, but cool the cat is smart enough to flip the lock."

"See? He's doin' it on purpose." Gina wagged her finger at him and turned to Autumn. "You must be Autumn. I've heard all about you."

Autumn shook her hand. "And you're Gina, Paulie's wife. Nice to meet you."

"Same here. I better head back downstairs," Gina said. "Paulie is probably wondering what happened to me."

"See ya later," Mercedes waited until Gina closed the door behind her before grabbing the Tupperware container, filled with Italian cookies and placing them on the dining room table. "You wanna Coke?"

"Sure." Autumn eyed the container of cookies. "What are these?"

"Ma's Italian cookies. They're delish." Mercedes carried two cans of Coke to the table and popped the tabs while Autumn reached inside the cookie container, and grabbed two. "I'm not sure how successful my joining the group was. I only heard your name once, in the beginning, when they told me you were part of the group. Then later, one of them mentioned you were under investigation for murder and then the romance writer, I forgot her name already..."

"Stephanie," Mercedes prompted.

"Yeah. Stephanie said she wasn't sure you were gonna come back."

"I never said that," Mercedes said. "Besides, why would they go around telling a complete stranger someone in their group was being investigated for murder?"

"That's what the older dude said. You weren't there to defend yourself and they changed the subject."

"Well, at least I know Tom is on my side," Mercedes muttered. "Nothing else was said that caught your attention?"

"Nope." Autumn popped the last of the cookie in her mouth. "This frosting is the best. I can taste cream cheese and something else."

"Lemon zest. Ma's secret ingredient is lemon zest."

"The cookies almost melt in your mouth," Autumn said. "That reminds me. Earlier today, I was talking to my buddy who works down at the precinct. He said they're at a standstill in Jon Luis' murder investigation. They went through his apartment and storage unit and couldn't find anything."

"That's it." Mercedes slammed the palm of her hand on the table. "Let me go grab my phone." She darted out of the room, returning moments later with her cell phone in hand. "Check this out." Mercedes handed the phone to Autumn.

Autumn reached for another cookie as she studied the screen. "What am I looking at?"

"The weird looking key attached to the other key ring. I think it's for a storage unit. Why would Jon Luis keep a storage unit key with his other keys? Most people store stuff and then put the key somewhere for safekeeping."

Mercedes drummed her fingers on the table. "I need to find out where his storage unit is located."

"The police already searched it," Autumn said. "They said there was nothin' in there but a bunch of magazines and books..." Her voice trailed off.

"Books," Mercedes said. "We're onto something. Text your friend and ask him if he can tell you the name of the storage unit."

"Okay." Autumn pulled her cell phone from her pocket and tapped the screen. "We'll see what he says. I'm still hungry."

"We still have some leftover pizza," Mercedes said.

"Why didn't you tell me that?"

Mercedes shoved her chair back and headed into the kitchen where she reached inside the fridge and pulled out a pizza box before carrying it to the dining room table. "I have no idea where you put all this food."

Autumn lifted the lid, reached inside and grabbed a slice of pizza before taking a big bite. "All of this sleuthing is making me hungry." Her phone beeped and she picked it up, juggling a slice of pizza in one hand and her cell phone in the other. "He said the unit was at Southern

Savannah Storage over off MLK Boulevard. I know exactly where it's at."

"Ask him for the unit number," Mercedes said.

Autumn shook her head. "No way. He'll know we're going over there and if he thinks we're snooping around, he'll be forced to report us and I'll risk losing my contact."

"Crud," Mercedes stared out the window. "I have an idea on how to find out what unit it is and I'm sure one of my brothers, or maybe even you, can help me find a way inside."

Chapter 13

"You want me to go with you Mercedes?" Tony asked.

"Nah." Mercedes gazed at the entrance to the Southern Savannah Storage office and reached for the car door handle. "It'll look less suspicious if I go in by myself. Wish me luck."

"You got this." Autumn leaned over the front seat and patted Mercedes' arm. "Remember, you're a grieving niece who wants to look through her uncle's belongings before you head back home."

"Got it." Mercedes gave her brother and Autumn a thumbs-up and slid out of the car. She hurried to the front door and took a quick look back before stepping into the small lobby.

Mercedes approached the counter. "I'm hoping you can help me. My uncle, Jon Luis, recently passed. He rented a storage unit here and I was wondering if there was any way I could take a look inside the unit."

The man eyed her suspiciously. "I don't know who Jon Luis is, I mean, was. He's a popular guy. First, the cops are in here searching the unit and now you."

"I don't mean to bother you. I'm heading home tomorrow and hoped to check it out before I leave," she said. "What happens if the items inside the unit go unclaimed?"

"I gotta wait thirty days after the bill is unpaid to post a notice stating I plan to sell the contents to settle the debt. It won't be happenin' to this unit anytime soon. The renter paid a year in advance. If you got a key to the unit, I can't stop you from lookin' around inside. It's a free country."

"Well, there's the problem," Mercedes said. "I don't have the key."

"I can't let you in," the man bluntly said. "If you got a key, help yourself."

"But I'm leaving town soon," Mercedes said. "Please?"

"Sorry. Can't do it."

Mercedes' hands dropped to her side and she turned to go. "I'm going to search my uncle's place one more time tonight. Can you at least tell me what I'm looking for? Describe the key to me?"

"Sure. It's orange, oblong and has the unit number on it." The man paused as he tapped the keyboard in front of him. "It's unit D62."

"D62. I'm gonna see if I can find it." She thanked him and exited the building.

Mercedes slid into the passenger seat and reached for her seatbelt. She could see the man watching her through the store window. "D62, but we're gonna have to sneak back in. He's watchin' me like a hawk. He's already suspicious since the cops have already been here, checkin' out the unit."

"No problem." Tony backed out of the spot, drove to the exit and turned left, onto the street. "There's a back alley over here and the fence ain't too high. I noticed it when we drove by. We'll have to find a way in. It shouldn't be too difficult."

"Famous last words," Autumn said. "You got something to pick the lock on the unit?"

"Maybe," Tony said.

"If not, I brought this." Autumn held up a small plastic container. "I borrowed it from Steve. He has a storage unit across town. He lost his key and found this baby on the internet. Said it works like a charm and even showed me how to use it."

"We'll keep it as a backup," Tony said as he eased into an empty parking spot directly behind the storage units. "This is as close as we're gonna get. We'll have to hoof it from here."

The trio exited the car and approached the chain link fence that secured the perimeter of the property.

Tony shaded his eyes and gazed in both directions. "We're gonna have to find a way in."

They walked along the sidewalk, all the way to the corner, before turning around and retracing their steps.

When they reached the other corner, Mercedes spotted a gap in the fence. "Over there. It'll be a tight squeeze. I'll go first."

Tony and Autumn tugged on the corners of the fence while Mercedes slipped through the gap. "Piece of cake."

"You go next," Autumn said.

"Ladies first."

She shrugged. "Okay."

Mercedes pushed on one side of the fence while Tony pulled. Autumn slipped through the opening and joined Mercedes on the other side.

"On the count of three, we both push our side." Mercedes nodded at Autumn. "One, two, three."

Tony squeezed through the opening while the women pushed on the fence. His jacket caught on a jagged piece of metal. *Rip.*

He tugged on the jacket and it ripped even more before he was able to pull it loose. "Great. Good thing it wasn't my favorite jacket," Tony added sarcastically.

After a quick inspection of the damage, Tony led the way, along the perimeter of the fence. "What unit are we lookin' for?"

"D62," Mercedes said. "We're in section G. It's probably over this way." They strode across the back of the property, passing by a couple of cars parked in front of two end units. "We're close now."

When they reached the building marked "D," they turned right and walked along the front of the large single stall units until they reached a section of smaller units.

"This is it." Autumn knelt down to examine the lock. "Awesome. This is the exact same lock Steve has on his storage unit."

"I'll try first." Tony waved Autumn to the side and knelt down to inspect the lock. "I think I've got the perfect tool." He reached in his front pocket, pulled out a Swiss Army knife and extended the gutting blade. "Just a little twist here."

Tony eased the blade inside the opening and twisted the tip. Nothing happened. "I got another blade in here." He removed the gutting blade, snapped it back in the slot and flicked open a smaller blade, repeating the same steps. Again, nothing happened.

"Let me give it a try," Autumn said.

"Be my guest." Tony stepped to the side and Autumn moved closer. She popped the top of the plastic case, reached inside and pulled out a small angled piece of metal.

"Someone's coming," Mercedes hissed.

Bright headlights illuminated the side of the storage unit as a vehicle eased along the gravel strip of road. It slowed as it drew closer.

"I hope that's not the storage manager," Mercedes whispered, her heart pounding.

The trio watched as a vintage, woodgrain station wagon crept by. An elderly woman stared at them through the driver's side window and Autumn waved as she drove by.

The vehicle stopped at the end of the row of storage buildings and the woman slowly climbed out of her car. She kept one eye on them as she hurried to the door of one of the larger units. After unlocking the unit door, the woman gave them another hard stare and then disappeared inside.

"Awesome. Now we have Nosy Nellie two doors down." Mercedes wiped her brow. "Let's hurry up before she comes back out."

"I'm trying." Autumn quickly inserted the small tool inside the keyhole and twisted. "I don't get it. It worked like a charm on Steve's lock." She tried again, this time giving the tool a firm twist. "Great. It's not working."

"Let me try." Mercedes held out her hand.

Autumn dropped the tool into her friend's hand.

Mercedes dropped to her knees, so that she was eye level with the lock. She slid the tip of the tool into the lock and slowly spun it counter-clockwise. *Click.*

"Bingo." The lock popped open. Mercedes handed the tool to Autumn before sliding the bar to the left. Next, she tugged on the bottom of the door. "I think it's stuck."

"You gotta use a little muscle." Tony gave the door a hard tug and it rolled up.

"Thanks bro." Mercedes' heart sank as she peered into the murky darkness. "It looks empty."

"I brought a flashlight with me." Tony reached in his pocket, pulled out a small flashlight and turned it on. He shined the light around the unit. "There's stuff in here."

Propped against the right-hand wall was a small, one-seater kayak. Next to the kayak was a plastic paddle. In front of the kayak were several fishing boxes and an array of fishing poles.

"What are those?" Autumn pointed behind the kayak, at two long pieces of wood with a pattern etched on the front.

"They look like water skis," Tony said. "We got a similar set for sale in the pawnshop."

"Mr. Luis was quite the outdoorsman," Mercedes said. "I read in one of his biographies that he worked for a couple of years as a writer for

Lonely Planet publishing. It's one of the largest travel guidebook publishers in the world. He's traveled to some exotic locations to document his travels."

"That's cool," Autumn said. "I wonder what's over here." She zigzagged around a maze of stacked storage boxes, to the other side of the unit. "Hey. Over here. Check this out."

Chapter 14

Carlita studied the lock on the balcony door, flipping it back and forth while Grayvie arched his back, appearing to have only a mild interest in what Carlita was doing.

"I'm gonna have to change this lock or risk having to crawl through Rambo's doggie door if you lock me out," she scolded.

Grayvie lifted his tail and then leapt off the table before strutting across the wood floors and making his way into the kitchen.

"It's a good thing I'm nearly an expert at changing locks, thanks to Elvira." Carlita stepped over to her small dining room desk and added a patio door lock to her growing list of items she planned to purchase on her next shopping trip.

Carlita set the pen on top of the yellow pad and headed into the kitchen when she heard a soft knock on the front door. "Wonder who that is." She peeped through the peephole and spotted Shelby standing on the other side.

Carlita swung the door open. "Hello Shelby."

"Hello Carlita. I'm sorry to bother you."

"You're never a bother."

The sound of loud voices followed by a dull *thunk* echoed in the hall. "Is Elvira at it again? I swear that woman can't move out of here fast enough."

Shelby's eyes widened. "Elvira is moving?"

"Yes. It's been so hectic around here; since Gina and my grandkids arrived, I haven't had time to tell you and Cool Bones that Elvira is moving out."

"That's why I'm here." Shelby clasped her hands. "I think Paulie and his wife are in the midst of a heated argument. I can hear them through the floor vents. I-I hesitate to say anything because it's none of my business, but then I heard one of the kids crying..." Her voice trailed off.

"Ne ho fin sopra i capelli." Carlita patted her head.

Shelby chuckled. "Did you just swear?"

"No. I said I'm sick and tired of their fighting." Carlita stepped into the hall, closing the door behind her. "It's their hot-blooded Italian tempers. I'm sorry if they're bothering you. I'll go tell them to lower their voices."

Shelby followed Carlita to the top of the stairs. "Violet has been asking if the kids can come over to play. If...your son and his wife need a break, you can send the kids up for a while. We've been playing board games and Violet would love someone besides me to play with."

"You're a doll." Carlita squeezed Shelby's arm. "I'm sure the kids would be thrilled."

"Perfect. I'll leave my front door open. Bring them on up," Shelby said.

Carlita hurried down the stairs and a loud crash, followed by angry voices echoed in the hall. She rapped sharply on the outer door. "Paulie? Gina?"

The door flew open and a red-faced Gina stood on the other side. She sucked in a breath and smoothed her hair. "Yes?"

"We can hear you yellin' and bangin' around through the floor vents. You need to tone it down before the neighbors call the cops."

"It wouldn't be the first time," Gina muttered. "Paulie and I are workin' on ironing out some issues."

"Iron them out or pound them into the ground?" Carlita shook her head. "Never mind. Shelby and Violet invited the kids to come upstairs and play."

PJ peeked around his mother's leg. "Can we go Ma?"

Gina ruffled her son's hair. "Yeah. It'll be a lot more fun than stayin' inside this tiny apartment." She took a step back. "Noel and Gracie? You wanna go play upstairs with Violet?"

"Who is Violet?" Noel skipped to the door.

"She's Nonna's friend," Gina explained.

"Okay," Noel said.

"I'll bring them back later," Carlita said. "In the meantime, you and Paulie work on whatever you got to, but keep it to a dull roar. We don't need the cops on our doorstep any more than they already are."

"Sorry Carlita." Gina rolled her eyes. "It's Paulie's temper."

"You *both* come by it rightfully. Vinnie and I used to fight like cats and dogs." She smiled softly. "Eventually, we got too old to fight. It wasn't worth it anymore." Carlita patted her daughter-in-law's arm. "You'll get tired of fighting one day. In the meantime, keep the lines of communication open and you'll be able to work it out."

"Can we go now Nonna?" PJ asked.

"Yes, we can go." Carlita took his hand. "Violet has board games you can play and maybe later, if you're on your best behavior at Violet's house, I'll take all of you over to A Scoop in Time for more ice cream."

She turned to Gina. "You tell Paulie to behave himself or his Ma is gonna come back down here and knock some sense into both of you."

Carlita stepped into the hall. "Come along my patatinos."

"I'm not a potato," Gracie wrinkled her nose. "I'm a girl."

"Then you're a bambolina," Carlita said.

"PJ is a patino," Noel giggled.

"Patatino," Carlita corrected. The children followed Carlita up the steps and to Shelby's door where she knocked lightly. "We're here."

Shelby appeared in the doorway. "Great. Violet has been bugging me ever since I mentioned the kids coming over. Come on in. We're getting ready to play the game Mouse Trap."

Violet ran to her mother's side. "We can sit at the coffee table." The children disappeared into the living room.

"Thanks for taking the kids. I'm sure they'll have fun," Carlita said. "I want to invite you to dinner, so that you can meet Gina. What does your schedule look like later this week?"

"It's wide open," Shelby said. "Just give me a day or two heads up."

"Perfect. I'll plan a nice Italian family-style dinner with homemade pasta and other goodies."

"It sounds delicious." Shelby leaned her hip against the door. "What happened with Elvira? I'm guessing she did something to break her lease."

"Again," Carlita said. "This time, she almost burned the place to the ground."

"No way." Shelby's eyes widened. "I thought I smelled smoke the other day."

"She grew bored painting watercolors and began working on a bust of herself. Then, she decided it needed a little bronzing, so she took a blow torch to it."

"Inside her apartment?"

"Yes. She set the curtains on fire, ripped them off the wall to put the fire out and put a couple big holes in the drywall in the process." Carlita went on to tell her it was the last straw and that she'd served Elvira with eviction papers.

"I wonder where she's moving to."

"She rented some space in the building across the alley," Carlita said. "Maybe I'll turn the dinner party into a going away party for Elvira."

"An unconventional send-off for an unconventional tenant," Shelby said. "Are you going to rent her apartment out right away?"

"I don't know. I need to make sure Elvira is out lock, stock and barrel, first."

"Not a bad idea since Elvira is completely unpredictable. You never know what she's going to do next."

"Mommy, can we have a popsicle?" Violet appeared and began tugging on her mother's arm.

"Sure."

"I better let you take care of the kids. I'm right across the hall if you need anything," Carlita said. She thanked Shelby again, made her way back to her apartment and started to close the door when she heard Tony's apartment door open.

"Fine!" Paulie stepped out into the hall. "If that's how you're gonna act, then there's nothing left to discuss."

The door slammed in Paulie's face.

Carlita briefly closed her eyes before opening them again. "I hate to have to do this," she muttered under her breath before marching down the stairs to where her youngest son stood staring at the door. "I swore I was never gonna stick my nose in the middle of my kids' business, but these blowouts have got to stop."

She rapped loudly on Tony's apartment door and heard a muffled reply, but the door didn't open. Carlita turned the knob. The door was locked. She rapped again, this time louder.

The door flew open. "I told you to go away," Gina snarled and then realized Carlita was on the other side. "I thought you was Paulie."

"Like I told Paulie, I swore I was never gonna get in the middle of my kids' business, but you two need an intervention." Carlita grabbed her son's arm and dragged him into the apartment. She pushed Gina out of the way and kicked the door shut.

"Sit," she commanded. "Both of you."

Gina opened her mouth, as if to reply, and then quickly closed it when she noted the dark expression on her mother-in-law's face.

"Look at you two. You have three beautiful babies upstairs who need both of their parents. You're fightin' like there's a war to be won and both of you are bent on comin' out on top. You both gotta take a step back, cool off and think about what you're doin'."

Carlita began to pace, desperate to add something that would sink in.

"She..."

"He..."

"Uh." Carlita held up a hand. "What's the big beef? One at a time and ladies first."

"Paulie says he don't wanna be mayor of Clifton Falls. He's ready for a career change and he wants to either open up the internet café in New York or move down here, to start over. I'm sayin' it's a big mistake. His job as mayor means a guaranteed income, security, a pension, health insurance."

"Okay. Paulie, it's your turn."

"Gina doesn't understand the job is a big burnout. I hate politics and I gotta go through the re-election process next year. I'm not lookin' forward to the mudslinging mess again."

"You've only served one term, Paulie," Gina said. "How do you know it will be a mudslinging mess?"

"Let Paulie finish," Carlita said.

"I've done my time and wanna move on. The internet café would give us a comfortable living. We're young. We gotta take chances now. Or, we can move to Savannah. The pawnshop is doin' real good. If Ma opens the restaurant, there will be more than enough work to go around, plus we'll have a place to live."

"This place is too small," Gina said.

She had a point.

"Why don't you compromise?" Carlita suggested. "I've got an idea. Paulie has another year before the next election. Let him partner up with…"

"Dino. Dino Scarpa," Paulie said.

"A made man if I ever met one," Gina muttered.

"Do you know that for certain?" Carlita asked.

"No, but I can tell, just by lookin' at him."

"Say he's not mafia. Paulie keeps his position as mayor and dabbles in the internet café with Dino as a side business, after checking to make sure Dino is not in "the family." If it doesn't work out, if he can't put food on the table and keep a roof over your head, Paulie runs for a second term as mayor."

Gina silently examined her fingernails while Paulie gazed pleadingly at his wife. "Please Gina? I won't bug you again about movin' to Savannah."

"You both gotta be willing to compromise," Carlita said.

"Okay," Gina finally caved. "We go back to New York; you don't breathe a word about not running for a second term. Let me check Dino out first and then if he's clean, you can hammer out a partnership...a six-month agreement to start."

"It's a deal." Paulie reached for his wife's hand.

Carlita patted Gina's shoulder and headed to the door. "Now I'm gonna get outta here, so you two can kiss and make up."

Chapter 15

Autumn hurried over to the left hand side of the storage unit. "Check out these bookshelves. They're full of books." She ran her hand along the edge of the shelf and a plume of dust filled the air.

Mercedes slid in next to Autumn and studied the books. "It's like a mini library in here. Jon Luis must not have had room for all of these in his apartment and couldn't bear to part with them."

"Some of these look old." Mercedes eased a book from the shelf and studied the cover. *How to Make Friends and Influence Enemies.*

"Here's one," Autumn said. "How to investigate a crime scene online."

"Oh. That's sounds interesting," Mercedes said. "I might have to track that one down."

"The clock is ticking ladies." Tony tapped the face of his watch. "If Mr. Storage Manager decides to check on the units, he's gonna catch us."

"True." Mercedes slid the book back on the shelf and opened the lower cabinet drawers, which was full of books. Each cabinet was the same and nothing stood out. "This is a bust. There's nothing in here but a bunch of books."

"And outdoor equipment," Autumn said.

"Right." Mercedes had started to close the cabinet at the end when something caught her eye. "What's this?" She pulled out a clear plastic bin. Inside the bin were several books, each stored in a Ziploc baggie. "Check this out."

She set the bin on top of the shelf, opened the lid and pulled out the top plastic bag. Mercedes held it up to the light. "*Crime in Corporate America* by JL Cordele." She carefully placed the book on the shelf, reached into the bin again and lifted the second book, *The Death Club* by JL Cordele, out.

There was one more book, *Savannah's Mysteries Revealed* by JL Cordele, in the bin.

"JL Cordele...Jon Luis," Mercedes waved the book in the air. "Jon Luis is JL Cordele. He wrote these books under a different name." Her hand trembled as she pulled out her cell phone, switched it to camera mode and took several pictures of the front and back covers of the books.

She opened the cover of the book and then flipped to the back, *About the Author*. She took a quick picture of the author page.

"I saw a guy walking around," Tony said. "He turned down one of the other aisles. I think it's the guy from the storage rental office and he's makin' his rounds."

Mercedes had slipped the first book back into the baggie, zipped it shut and started to set it inside the bin when she noticed a fourth baggie. Inside the baggie was a thick stack of papers, clipped together. "I found something else." She snatched the stack of papers from the bin, tucked them under her arm before placing the books inside the bin and snapping it shut. "Let's go."

Autumn and Mercedes ran out of the unit and Tony pulled the door down, snapping the lock in place. "Just in time. He's comin' this way."

The trio strode to the end of the row of storage units, veered left and then jogged to the corner of the property. Tony pushed on the fence while the women squeezed through the opening and then they held it for him while he slipped out.

"Hey!" The man began running toward them. Mercedes recognized him as the man she'd spoken with earlier in the office.

The trio picked up the pace and ran to the end of the block.

They hopped into the Tony's car and Mercedes yanked her door shut. "That was a close one."

"Close only counts in horseshoes and hand grenades," Autumn joked. "Seriously, I think you're onto something. JL Cordele. I guess we shoulda figured Jon Luis might have used another name."

"Yeah," Mercedes said, "It makes sense."

Tony sped off and made a quick turn down a side street before turning onto the main road. He glanced into his rearview mirror. "I think we're bein' tailed."

"You do?" Mercedes started to turn around.

"Don't look back. They might see you. I'll make a few more turns to see if we're being followed." Tony swerved to the right and turned onto a one-way street.

Mercedes glanced in the side mirror. "He's still back there."

"Yep. Hang on." Tony made a quick left and the car followed. "I wish I woulda been paying attention when we left the storage place." They drove up and down several side streets and the car continued to tail them.

"Let's drive to the police station," Mercedes said.

"I got a gun in the glove box," Tony said. "Get it out, just in case."

Mercedes reached inside the glove box and pulled out a small handgun. She set it on the seat between them. "I'll let you do the shooting. You gonna drive to the police station?"

"Yeah. If I was by myself, I'd pull over and see what's up, but I'm not gonna put my baby sister and friend in harm's way." Tony drove to the other side of Savannah and pulled into the police station parking lot. The car followed them into the parking lot and pulled into an empty spot next to them.

They watched as Detective Wilson climbed out of the vehicle, an unmarked police car, and approached the passenger side window.

Mercedes rolled down the window and the detective leaned in. "Mercedes Garlucci. Why am I not surprised to see you?"

"I've got a bigger question. Why am I surprised to see you?"

"Got a call from Roland, over at Southern Savannah Storage. He said some woman was snooping around, asking questions about Jon Luis' storage unit. Then he noticed someone out in front of the unit and he gave me a call. Wanna tell me what that's all about?" the detective asked.

Mercedes casually slid Tony's gun under her leg. "I'm trying to find out who murdered Jon Luis before you throw the cuffs on and haul an innocent woman - me - off to jail."

"This is an official investigation. We don't need your help."

"Well, apparently you do," Mercedes snipped. "Otherwise you wouldn't be harassing me."

Detective Wilson shook his head. "At the very least, you're putting yourselves in danger, trying to track down a killer."

"Point taken," Mercedes said. "We'll be on our way."

Without another word of warning, the detective returned to his car and followed them out of the parking lot. Mercedes was certain he was going to follow them all the way home, but he turned onto the main thoroughfare, leading out to the highway.

"I have a feeling the friendly detective is gonna be keepin' an eye out for us," Tony said.

"Yeah, I wouldn't be surprised if he does." Mercedes stared out the window. "I need to do more research on JL Cordele. I'm certain it's Jon Luis, using another pen name. And I still think someone in my author group set me up. We need to come up with a plan to flush them out."

She shifted in her seat. "A trap." Mercedes snapped her fingers. "This is perfect. Autumn, you told the group you worked at the Savannah Evening News, right?"

"Yes, and I'm sorry I did. They asked me to find copy editors for them."

"Well, I'm glad you did. I think JL Cordele is going to help us move this investigation along. We need to put our heads together, to come up with a plan, set a trap and flush out the killer."

When Tony stopped in front of Autumn's apartment, Mercedes thanked her for bringing the lock-picking tool and for going undercover to spy on the other authors.

"No problem. You would do the same for me." Autumn slid out of the back seat and hopped onto the sidewalk. "Let me know if you need me to go to the meeting next week. I think I can stay awake this time."

"Thanks, Autumn." Mercedes gave her a thumbs-up. "You're the best."

Chapter 16

As soon as Mercedes and Tony arrived home, Mercedes headed to her computer to start researching JL Cordele. She settled into her chair, clicked on the search bar and typed in Jon Luis Cordele, but found nothing.

"Maybe it's JL Cordele," she whispered. She typed in JL Cordele and several book images popped up on the screen.

Mercedes reached for her cell phone, clicked on the camera icon and scrolled through the pictures she'd taken inside the storage unit. The book names were the same.

She set her phone on the desk and then clicked on JL Cordele's biography. The biography was a goldmine of information. JL Cordele was born and raised in Augusta, Georgia. After graduating from Augusta University, with a bachelor's degree in criminal justice, he moved to Savannah, Georgia to start his career as a fraud investigator.

JL Cordele became bored and after working on a case involving a group of Savannah area businessmen, he discovered that he enjoyed writing about criminals more than investigating them. The men had overinflated their company's profit numbers to shareholders and fudged the company's expense reports.

The biography stated Cordele was intrigued with the minds of individuals who committed such crimes and penned his first novel, *Crime in Corporate America.* After the first book published and received critically acclaimed reviews, he began to delve deeper into the prominent and powerful families of Savannah and wrote the book, *The Death Club.*

By the time JL Cordele penned his third book, *Savannah's Mysteries Revealed,* he was receiving death threats, left the area and went into hiding.

Mercedes stared blankly at the screen. Although the information never stated JL was "Jon Luis," she was convinced they were the same person. Had Jon Luis returned to Savannah and the people who threatened to kill him years ago found out? She thought about her lunch date with Zachary and him telling her that Jon Luis' apartment had been ransacked.

Her author group knew Jon Luis was in Savannah. If they knew about it, others must, as well. A chill ran down her spine. That meant there was also a good chance they knew Mercedes planned to meet with Jon Luis. Was the killer's goal to end Jon Luis' book research? Was she the next target?

Jon Luis must've known the background of George Delmario, which meant if he'd dug around enough he knew, or at least suspected, the Garlucci family had ties to "the family."

Mercedes opened another browser screen and Amazon to see if she could purchase an e-book copy of *The Death Club* and found it was only available in paperback. It was the same for *Savannah's Mysteries Revealed*. She didn't have time to wait for paperback copies to ship. She could be dead by the time they arrived.

Unless…Mercedes logged onto the Savannah District Library's website and began searching for books by JL Cordele. *Crime in Corporate America* wasn't listed in the system. She found *Savannah's Mysteries Revealed* was checked out, so she began searching for *The Death Club*. The book showed it was available.

Mercedes grabbed her phone and purse and headed into the living room where her mother sat watching television. "I'm going to the library to pick up a book by JL Cordele. Do you want to go with me?"

Carlita set the remote in her lap. "I have to hang around here in case Shelby needs help with the kids."

"PJ, Noel and Gracie are next door?"

"Yes, Shelby offered to let them come play with Violet while Paulie and Gina spend time alone together."

"Is everything okay? I heard loud voices coming from Tony's place earlier and he told me Gina and Paulie were fighting like cats and dogs."

"I think they're finally starting to work through their disagreements, with a little motherly and mother-in-law butting in, as much as I didn't wanna do it," Carlita said. "Let's just say they're trying to hammer out a compromise and they better work it out or I'm gonna knock a couple heads together."

Mercedes grinned. "I'm sure you will. Remind me to never fight with my husband in front of you - if I ever get married, that is."

***

The library was only a few squares away, so Mercedes decided to walk. It was a beautiful day and the fresh air gave her time to mull over the clues. If she could only figure out a way to confirm JL Cordele and Jon Luis were the same person.

After JL Cordele started receiving death threats, he must have decided to start writing under the name Jon Luis. Still, writing about unsolved murder mysteries under the name Jon Luis would potentially make him a target, and Mercedes suspected that was why his public biography and personal information for author Jon Luis were vague.

JL or Jon Luis' killer could've been any number of people. It would take Mercedes time to study his books and search for clues, and even if she did, there was still no guarantee she would be able to figure out who murdered Jon Luis.

She thought about the people in her author group, trying to remember who had first mentioned Jon Luis' name. When she reached the library, Mercedes still couldn't recall who had brought his name up.

She stopped in front of the magnificent historic building. Mercedes had passed by the library many times, but never stopped. She knew it was old and had seen a blurb online that the library, built in 1916, recently celebrated its one-hundredth birthday.

After restoring the library to its former glory and doubling the original size to an impressive 66,000 square feet, the city changed the name from the Bull Street Library to the Live Oak Public Library. Mercedes suspected it had something to do with the towering live oak trees surrounding it.

She ascended the sets of steps and walked between the massive white Georgia marble columns as she entered the library.

Mercedes paused to appreciate the beauty of the building as she gazed around. The murmur of soft voices echoed in the hall as she made her way to the information desk. "Yes, I'm here to track down a book."

The woman behind the desk smiled. "Do you have a library card?"

"Not yet."

"No problem. We can get you set up. Do you have a picture ID?"

Mercedes reached into her pocket, pulled out her wallet and handed the woman her driver's license. After the woman entered her information in the computer, she handed Mercedes her ID and new library card. "What book can I help you find?"

Mercedes gave the woman the name of the book.

"Follow me." The librarian led her to the non-fiction mystery section where she plucked a book from one of the shelves and handed it to Mercedes. "Is this it?"

"The Death Club. Perfect. Thank you," Mercedes said.

The woman accompanied Mercedes back to the front desk. "This is a popular book today. This branch only carries two copies of *The Death Club*. The other copy was checked out this morning."

She continued. "Now that you have a library card, you can reserve books online." The woman scanned the book before she tucked a receipt inside the cover and slid the book across the desk. "The return date is on your receipt. You should check out our library before you go. We have over 500,000 items. You can download e-stuff, like e-books, audio and videos, plus we have a whole bank of computers available to residents."

"I'm kind of on a tight schedule today," Mercedes said. "I'll be sure to come back when I have more time. I love libraries." She thanked the woman for her help and exited the library.

When she returned home, her mother was gone and the apartment was quiet. Mercedes settled onto the sofa and began reading. *The Death Club* was a fascinating story with a preface about JL

Cordele's research. While she read, she jotted down several of the names he mentioned, so she could research them later.

After reading for a couple of hours, Mercedes realized that if she researched every single person in the book, and she'd only made it a quarter of the way through it, she'd be researching for weeks.

Frustrated, she tucked the receipt between the chapters where she'd left off and slammed the book shut. "Ugh. This is going to take me forever. There has to be a better way."

Mercedes grabbed a pillow and covered her face. She was in the same position when her mother returned to the apartment a short time later.

"Hey," Carlita lifted the corner of the pillow. "You feelin' all right?"

"No. I'm depressed. I feel like I'm running around in circles. I have no idea who murdered Jon Luis." Mercedes uncovered her face. "I'm almost certain JL Cordele and Jon Luis are the same person, but based on what I've read in this book, any number of people could've taken him out. All of the people he wrote about...they can't all be dead."

Carlita perched on the edge of the chair and stared at her daughter thoughtfully. "Remember how Tierney Grant told us Jon Luis contacted her about the Honeycutt / Madison Square murder? I don't think it was a coincidence he wanted to meet with you. He even jotted your name and address on a notepad. I think he was lookin' for info on George Delmario."

"If we could figure out who was involved in the third case..." Mercedes sat up. "Wait a minute. I took a bunch of papers from Jon Luis' storage unit. They were clipped together and in a plastic bag. I thought that maybe it was part of a manuscript. I forgot about them after Detective Wilson stopped us."

"The bag is still in the car." Mercedes sprang from the sofa and ran down to the pawnshop.

Tony was at the desk, working on the computer.

"I need your car keys."

"What's up?" Tony reached into the top drawer and pulled out a set of keys before tossing them to his sister.

"Remember that bag I took, er, I mean borrowed from Jon Luis' storage unit? I left it in your car and completely forgot about it after the detective followed us. It's still in your car. I'll be right back." Mercedes stepped into the hall.

"Don't forget to lock it," Tony called out after her.

Mercedes found the bag right where she'd left it, and after locking the car, she returned to the pawnshop and handed Tony his keys.

"You found it?"

"Yep." Mercedes waved the papers in the air. "I can't believe I forgot all about it."

"Well, bein' followed by the fuzz probably rattled you, not to mention being chased out of the storage place by the manager."

"Right?" Mercedes thanked her brother again and then returned to the apartment. "I got it."

"Great," Carlita said. "What is it?"

"Jon Luis aka JL Cordele's manuscript." Mercedes sat on the sofa, tucking her legs underneath her as she pulled the papers from the bag and unclipped them. "I found three JL Cordele books inside a plastic bin, along with this, written by Jon Luis. They're the same person."

"Well?" Carlita asked.

"This is definitely a manuscript." She quickly flipped through the pages. "*Unsolved Murders in Savannah: Mafia Ties, White Lies and Rush Into Murder. The Cold Case Files* by Jon Luis."

Mercedes tapped the top with the tips of her fingers. "Why was it in the bin? If Jon Luis was working on it, why would he hide it in a storage unit?" She remembered how they'd spotted the storage unit keys, along with other keys, next to Jon Luis' body.

"Didn't you say that the young detective, Mr. Jackson, told you Jon Luis reported his apartment had been ransacked shortly before his death?" Carlita asked. "Maybe he was hiding the manuscript in the storage unit."

"You're right, Ma. That makes perfect sense. Someone is desperate to get their hands on this," Mercedes said. "And I'm itching to read it!"

"I'll make some coffee." Carlita wandered into the kitchen. After the coffee brewed, she poured a cup for Mercedes and set it on the end table, next to the sofa.

Rambo began to whine, so he and Carlita headed out for a long walk down by the river.

Mercedes' nose was still buried in the manuscript when they returned, so Carlita headed across the hall to check on her grandchildren and then down to the pawnshop to see if Tony and their part-time employee needed any help.

When she returned to the apartment, she found Mercedes pacing the floor. The manuscript was lying on top of the coffee table.

"It's just as I suspected. Jon Luis, aka JL Cordele, started this book after returning to Savannah. He was working on solving the Honeycutt murder, as well as Delmario's murder. Somehow, he linked us to Delmario and possibly to the family."

Carlita began to feel lightheaded and reached for the back of the chair to steady herself. "Will this never end? I wonder if Jon Luis shared his suspicions with anyone else."

"I don't know. *Unsolved Murders in Savannah: Mafia Ties, Rush Into Murder and White Lies. The Cold Case Files.*, is about three separate, high profile unsolved murder cases. Mafia ties is about George Delmario. White Lies is about the Madison Square / Herbert Honeycutt's murder. According to Luis' notes, he didn't have all of the puzzle pieces in place. His theory was Mrs. Honeycutt lied to protect her husband's killer."

"And the third one?" Carlita asked.

"Rush Into Murder is about Warren Paulson. Warren and his family lived here in Savannah and Warren's family was involved in local politics. According to the few notes Jon Luis jotted down, Warren was a bit of a wild card. He'd drifted from job to job until he landed a position as a defense contractor. Luis' theory was that the family pulled some strings to get him the position. Not long after getting the job, rumors began circulating that Warren was selling satellite secrets to Russian spies."

"Wow. It sounds like the makings of a movie," Carlita said.

"Or the beginning of a great story," Mercedes said. "It gets even better. According to Jon Luis, the feds were turning up the heat on Warren and word began to circulate that Warren was getting ready to rat out his Russian contacts. Right afterwards, Warren went missing. The investigators discovered his fishing boat was missing from the marina so the Coast Guard was sent out to search for him. They eventually found Warren Paulson's boat, but there was no sign of Paulson."

"The Russians took him out," Carlita whispered. "No wonder Jon Luis is dead. He was digging into an espionage case."

"Which was either really brave or really dumb." Mercedes continued. "Jon Luis believed the Russians paid Warren tens of thousands of dollars."

Carlita sipped her coffee. "Let me guess. The Coast Guard never found Warren's body."

"Nope." Mercedes shivered. "He's probably at the bottom of the ocean or ended up being fish food."

"You still think there's a link to your author group?" Carlita asked. "Do any of them speak Russian or have Russian ties?"

"I have no idea. Let's just say the killer or killers, either Herbert Honeycutt's killer or the Russian spies, found out Luis' was workin' on a new book, so they set into motion a plan to take out Luis and frame one of the potential suspects...me."

"Could be 'the family' from up north, too," Carlita pointed out.

"True, but here's the reason I'm leaning towards someone that's an author or in my author group." Mercedes turned to the last page of the manuscript. "Check out Luis' handwritten notes. He wrote in here he suspected someone knew about the manuscript, although he hadn't told anyone, other than mentioning it to his agent and the book publisher."

"So maybe you can link the killer via the publisher." Carlita sank into the chair. "That's gonna be tricky."

"Tricky, but not impossible and I'm hoping Autumn can help." Mercedes tugged on a stray strand of hair. "The group already knows that Autumn works for the newspaper and is writing a book. I could ask her if she'll go to this week's meeting and tell them she's looking for a publisher and see if she gets a bite."

"It's a stretch, Mercedes."

"What other choice do we have?"

"None," Carlita said. "None other than waiting for Detective Wilson to look into Luis' manuscript, figure out George Delmario was murdered on our property and the man who was researching the book, the man you were meeting, was found dead."

"Like I said, someone managed to pull off the perfect setup," Mercedes said. "But it ain't gonna stick to Mercedes Garlucci, not if I have a say in it."

Chapter 17

"Let's go over this one more time," Mercedes said. "What's the name of your space opera book?"

"Zebulon Galaxy: The Final Frontier. Why did I have to pick such a stupid genre?" Autumn groaned.

"That's a matter of opinion. Space Opera is very popular. You can make a lot of money writing sci-fi books."

"They're not gonna believe I forgot to bring my manuscript again," Autumn said. "What author joins an author's group and never remembers to bring their manuscript?"

"I've got you covered. One sec." Mercedes held up a finger and ran to her room, returning moments later carrying a manila file folder. "I put this together earlier today. Here's your manuscript."

"You wrote a space opera book?" Autumn flipped the folder open.

"I started a space opera draft. It's only a few chapters, enough so that the others won't be suspicious. It's what you told me – it's about two families who fled planet earth and arrive in Zebulon. Right now they're on the run, trying to avoid being eaten by Nancrites, the carnivorous creatures, which live on Zebulon and drink human blood."

"That's great and gross. Nancrites," Autumn repeated. "What if they want more details?"

"Ask them if they would like to read a copy. Tell them you're too nervous to talk about it." Mercedes guided her friend down the stairs and into the alley. "Your main goal is to tell them you're considering sending your manuscript to a publisher and are looking for suggestions."

"And who are you looking for?"

"Jon Luis' publisher is, I mean was, The Batton Group."

"Got it." Autumn circled her thumb and forefinger and gave her an A-OK before easing her helmet on and fastening the strap. "I'll be back before you know it." She tucked the file folder and manuscript inside her backpack and slipped it on.

When Autumn reached *The Book Nook*, she hurried inside, waving to Tillie on her way to the meeting room where Tom Muldoon, Austin Crawford and Cricket Tidwell were waiting. Stephanie wasn't there.

Cricket turned when she caught a glimpse of Autumn darting through the doorway. "You made it. We were wondering if you were going to show up."

"I'm a little late." Autumn eased into an empty seat. "I was halfway here and realized I forgot my manuscript." She pulled the file folder from her backpack and set it on the table. "Is the other woman coming?"

"Yes. Stephanie is on her way. Ah, there she is," Tom said.

"Sorry I'm late." The woman hurried into the room. "My car battery died and I had to get a jump. I'll probably need another one to get home."

She dropped her papers on the desk. "Hi Autumn. Glad you could make it."

The group began to discuss the progress they'd made on their manuscripts the previous week. Austin was almost done with his first read through on his next book. Tom told the group he'd finished publishing his new book two days earlier and planned to take some time off.

Cricket reported she'd started a spring cookbook she hoped to have finished by early February. "What about you Stephanie?"

She rolled her eyes. "Harlequin wants me to write another in my Charlotte Laine Regency Series."

"What's wrong with that?" Austin asked.

"Nothing, I suppose. The money is good. My problem is that I can't stand the main character. I'm thinking of killing her off."

"You can't do that," Cricket said. "It will be career suicide, especially if your readers are attached to her. What's her problem?"

"She's too nice, too sweet...syrupy sweet."

"Maybe you could give her some sort of contagious illness," Autumn suggested. "That way, you can cause her to be bedridden and then segue one of the other characters, one that you do like, into playing a larger part in the book."

"Great idea," Stephanie grinned. "That might work. How about you?"

"It's a slow go," Autumn said. "Maybe I picked the wrong genre." She patted the file folder. "I brought my draft with me in case anyone wants to check it out. I was thinking that maybe it's time for me to start researching publishers. Does anyone have a suggestion?"

Austin lifted a hand. "I'm indie all the way. Publishers take too much of your money."

"I'm no help," Stephanie said. "The Harlequins are traditionally published through their own company."

"I had a publisher," Tom said. "I'm going indie this time around. Austin is right. They want too much of your money, plus I would never recommend mine, so I'm of no help."

Autumn turned to Cricket.

"I'm traditionally published, what with cook books and such; there are too many photographs for mine to look good going it alone. My publisher handles mostly non-fiction."

"What's the name?" Autumn asked.

"It doesn't matter," Cricket shook her head. "They won't even look at space opera books."

"Try researching ABoards on line. It's an author's forum and they have some great tips and info for newbies," Austin suggested.

"Awesome," Autumn jotted the name on the inside of the file folder. "Thanks for the tip."

The group discussed their works, offering suggestions to the others and Autumn was proud she was able to add her two cents, based on her experience as a copy editor and employee of the local paper.

The meeting flew by and finally it was time to go. Desperate to give it one more shot, Autumn reached for her file folder. "No one has any suggestions on publishers?"

They all shook their heads.

"When you gonna invite us out to your ranch?" Austin turned to Tom. "I drove by it last week, on my way to a friend's place. I remember you telling me what road it was on. It has your monogrammed initials on the gate, right?"

"Yeah. TM. I'll invite ya'll over maybe next month," Tom said.

"We can meet at my place, too," Stephanie said. "It's kinda cramped but in a great location, not far from the Savannah Civic Center. There's a nice pub-type restaurant below our apartment. We could meet for dinner."

"That sounds like fun," Cricket said. "Although I don't mind having it here, a change of scenery might be nice."

"I might be able to make it too," Autumn said. "I've been working a little overtime. We're down a copy editor and looking for a replacement, but I would be interested."

"Maybe Mercedes will be back by then," Cricket said. "I should give her a call to check in. I'm starting to grow concerned."

"Maybe she fled to Canada. New York isn't too far from there," Stephanie said.

"I hope I get a chance to meet her," Autumn fibbed. "What does she write again?"

"Mafia, mobsters, mystery," Tom said. "We like to joke around with her that she seems to know an awful lot about it. Course she is from New York and all."

"It sounds interesting." Autumn thanked them again for including her in the group, slowly walked out of the store and stepped onto the sidewalk. She was no closer to helping her friend figure out who might have set her up than when she'd walked in.

Autumn hopped on her Segway and sped to the end of the street. She paused when she reached the corner, teetering to keep her balance as she adjusted her backpack when she caught a glimpse of someone coming up behind her. She shifted to the side to get a better look, and the person stepped into a doorway and out of sight. *Stop with the paranoia Autumn,* she scolded herself.

She tightened the straps and, after making sure her cell phone was secure, turned onto Mercedes' side street and steered her Segway into the alley behind the apartment before she hopped off. She spotted a movement up on the balcony. It was Mercedes. "How'd it go?"

Autumn shook her head. "I'll tell ya in a minute."

She parked the Segway near the stoop and waited for Mercedes to open the door.

"It was a bust," she blurted out. Autumn repeated the conversation and how not one single person divulged their publisher's name.

"Are you sure Austin said he was indie all the way?" Mercedes asked. "He told me he once had a publisher."

"That's what he said, unless I misunderstood him."

"And Stephanie said she's an indie author except for her romance books?"

"Those are published by Harlequin," Autumn nodded. "Tom said his wasn't good and Cricket said hers publishes *mostly* non-fiction, but she wouldn't give me their name."

"Maybe they're lying," Mercedes said. "Maybe their publishers are awesome and they want to keep them to themselves. I guess it would be smart for me to double check online, too."

"I did think one thing was interesting," Autumn said. "Didn't you say Stephanie moved to Savannah not long ago?"

"Right."

"The others, they've all lived in the area for a while."

"Yep," Mercedes confirmed.

"What if Stephanie writes romance as a cover? What if she followed Jon Luis to Savannah?"

"Maybe," Mercedes wrinkled her nose. "I gotta find out which one of these people published with The Batton Group."

"What if Jon Luis / JL Cordele published with more than one publisher?"

"It could be." Mercedes sighed heavily. "It appears I need to do a little more background research into Jon Luis / JL Cordele's writing career."

Mercedes thanked her friend for trying and watched as she hopped on her Segway and headed out onto the sidewalk. She was close to figuring out who had murdered Jon Luis, who had set her up, so close and yet so far.

She needed to find someone in the author group she could trust, someone she was certain had not been the one to set her up.

Chapter 18

Mercedes strode into *The Book Nook* and made her way to the counter in the back. "Is Cricket here?"

"Not yet." The young man behind the counter shook his head. "She should be in around one this afternoon. Is there something I can help you with?"

"No, I need to talk to her. Could you please leave her a message, tell her Mercedes stopped by and I'll be back later this afternoon?"

"Sure." The man reached for a pen and scribbled on a Post-it before peeling it off and sticking it on the back of the counter. "She's popular this morning. I got a whole list of people trying to track her down."

"If you talk to her, tell her it's not an emergency," Mercedes said. "I just wanted to run something by her." She thanked the man, exited the bookstore and climbed into the car.

She was almost home when her cell phone rang. It was Cricket.

"Hello?"

"Hello Mercedes. I guess I just missed you. I have a note here that you stopped by to see me," Cricket said. "I didn't know you were back in town."

"I'm home," Mercedes said. "The man working at the bookstore said you wouldn't be in until early afternoon."

"I'm not scheduled to work until one. I stopped downstairs to pick up a couple of packages I need to mail and saw you were one of the people looking for me. I thought I would call you first since you took the time to come all the way over here."

"I…I wanted to run something by you," Mercedes said. "You sound busy."

Cricket cut her off. "I've taken care of most of my errands. I have to return a couple more phone calls but if you're in the area why don't you come back by? I'll make a pot of tea."

"Okay. I'll head back your way."

"Great. If you're standing in front of the bookstore, walk through the courtyard gate on the left-hand side and you'll see a set of steps. My apartment is at the top of the stairs."

"Thanks, Cricket." Mercedes turned the car around and headed back to the bookstore. When she reached *The Book Nook*, she parked the car out front, made her way into the courtyard, up the steps and knocked on the door at the top of the stairs.

Cricket opened the door and smiled at Mercedes. "Come in. It's nice to see you, Mercedes. I had no idea you were back in town."

A twinge of guilt filled Mercedes for fibbing to her friends. "I never left town," she confessed. "I didn't know what to say and didn't want to meet with the others these last few days."

Mercedes didn't elaborate and Cricket didn't ask. "We hope you'll join us again. We've missed you."

"Thanks. I've missed all of you, too."

"Would you care for a cup of tea? I just brewed it," Cricket said. "It's honey lavender and good for stress relief."

"Yes. Thank you. I could use some stress relief."

"Please. Have a seat." Cricket poured two cups and carried them to the small bistro table while Mercedes slipped into the chair near the door. "What brings you here? You sounded like you need to talk."

"I do. It's about Jon Luis' murder." Mercedes lifted the cup and the aroma of lavender swirled in the air as she took a sip. "I think the investigators believe I murdered Jon Luis. Have you ever heard of George Delmario?"

"I…" Cricket poured a packet of sugar in her cup and reached for her spoon. "Yes. George Delmario owned your property. He was murdered. His body was found out by the alley dumpster and the case was never solved."

"Have you heard the rumor he had mafia ties?" Mercedes asked softly.

"Yes." Cricket nodded. "I have a confession to make, too. The other authors, all of us, knew you and your family owned the property. Anyone who's lived in Savannah in the last decade knew about Delmario's murder and his alleged mafia ties. There was also a rumor about some gems."

"I see." Mercedes shifted in her seat. "I found out Jon Luis was in the process of working on another book, *Unsolved Murders in Savannah: Mafia Ties, White Lies and Rush Into Murder. The Cold Case Files.* The reason Jon Luis agreed to meet me was not to give me information about the Madison Square murder case, one of the cases he was working on, but to pump me for information about George Delmario's murder." She told Cricket the investigators not only found Mercedes' name, but also her address scribbled on a yellow pad they found on Jon Luis' desk.

Cricket's eyes widened. "And the other case?"

"I've almost figured out the third one and was hoping you could help."

"Maybe we should discuss it in our author group. If we put our heads together, we might be able to figure it out," Cricket said.

"The only problem is that I think Jon Luis' killer is someone in our group. This person set me up."

"Oh dear," Cricket clutched her chest. "That's hard to believe."

"Do you remember who brought up the subject of Jon Luis in the first place?" Mercedes asked. "For the life of me, I can't remember."

"No," Cricket shook her head. "I don't recall, either. Of course, we've discussed a lot of different cases since you write mystery, Tom writes thriller/suspense and Austin writes historical mysteries."

"Here's my theory. Someone knew Jon Luis was in the process of writing a book. Maybe he was getting close to cracking the cases. Luis already contacted Tierney Grant, the owner of the old Honeycutt Manor. He contacted me and set up a meeting to discuss George Delmario's murder, which means he may have already made contact with the person or persons involved in the third case, as well."

Mercedes went on to explain the killer or whoever was trying to keep the third case quiet, somehow knew Mercedes was part of Luis' book research. "Jon Luis also wrote several books under another pen name...JL Cordele."

"I've never heard the name," Cricket said. "Do you recall the names of his books? Maybe that will jog my memory."

"The books were older." Mercedes slipped her cell phone out of her pocket, switched it on and flipped through the pictures. "There are three books written by JL Cordele - *Crime in Corporate America, The Death Club* and *Savannah's Mysteries Revealed.*"

"None of those ring a bell. I do recall Jon Luis was receiving death threats years ago. That's why he left town and went into hiding," Cricket said.

Mercedes hesitated for a fraction of a second, wondering if she should tell Cricket she had a copy of the manuscript and decided she needed help. Cricket was her best bet. "I have the manuscript. I can't tell you how I got it, though."

"I probably don't want to know how you got it," Cricket said. "Do you have the details of the third mystery?"

"According to Jon Luis' notes, Rush Into Murder was about Warren Paulson, a Savannah resident whose family was involved in local politics. Warren bounced from job to job and was eventually hired as a defense contractor. Not long after taking the position, rumors began to circulate that he was selling sensitive satellite information to the Russians. Jon Luis believed that Warren was getting ready to turn over the names of his Russian contacts when he disappeared. His family filed a missing person's report and the investigators discovered Paulson's boat was gone from the marina. According to Jon Luis' research, Paulson went out on his boat, all alone and late at night and never returned. The Coast Guard eventually found Paulson's boat, but no sign of Paulson."

"So you're telling me that Luis managed to stir up a hornet's nest. He made contact with someone involved in either the Honeycutt or Warren Paulson case and that person ended up killing him," Cricket said, "and you're convinced this person is in our group?"

"Now that we've talked about it, I'm not sure," Mercedes said. "It seems like an awfully big coincidence everyone knew where and when I was meeting Jon Luis and then he ends up getting murdered at our meeting spot." She downed the last of her tea. "Thanks for letting me bounce my ideas off of you. I'm gonna head home and start digging around some more into Warren Paulson and the Russian connection."

She thanked Cricket again for the tea and stood. "I plan to be at this week's meeting."

Cricket walked her to the door. "I know you didn't kill Jon Luis. I'm not even sure I believe someone in our group killed Jon Luis. I'm going to go through my book inventory to see if I can find anything in stock written by either Jon Luis or JL Cordele."

On the trip home, Mercedes mulled over the Russian connection. Perhaps it wasn't someone in the author group. Maybe she'd just been in the wrong place at the wrong time.

She drove to the end of the block and headed past *Shades of Ink Tattoo* shop where she spotted Steve standing on the stoop and waved. One of these days, she needed to pop in to say 'hi' but not today. She had murder on her mind.

Mercedes turned into the alley and almost collided with a police car that was blocking the alley. She swerved around the car and spotted several uniformed officers digging through their dumpster.

Chapter 19

Carlita stood near the back of her building and watched as two men wearing white jumpsuits and rubber gloves rummaged through her trash bin. While the men searched the dumpster, two others stood on the other side holding trash bags. "You're not gonna find a single thing in our dumpster to implicate my daughter in Jon Luis' death."

"We'll be the judge of that," Detective Wilson said. "We have to follow up on every tip, every lead."

"You're gonna waste your time because some bozo called in an anonymous tip telling you Jon Luis' murder weapon was inside our dumpster," Carlita said. "Who would know that, other than the killer?"

"What if your daughter confided in a friend? There's a reward for information leading to an arrest. People turn in criminals all of the time."

Mercedes parked the car and hurried to her mother's side. "What's going on?"

"Someone called in a tip that Jon Luis' murder weapon was in our dumpster," Carlita said.

"That's crazy," Mercedes sputtered. "Only the killer would know where the murder weapon is."

"We've already gone over that. Detective Wilson seems to think you confided in someone, told them you tossed the weapon in the dumpster and they turned you in to collect a reward."

"Five grand." Detective Wilson shoved his hands in his pockets.

"You can't search our dumpster without a search warrant," Mercedes said.

"Your mother gave me permission."

"Because there isn't anything in there," Carlita said.

"We got something, Wilson." One of the men stuck a gloved hand in the air and began waving it.

"I'll be right back." The detective stepped off the stoop and hurried to the bin.

"Tell me this ain't happenin'," Mercedes groaned.

"I wish it wasn't." Carlita squinted her eyes. "Looks like a gun. Let's go."

Carlita and Mercedes jogged to Detective Wilson's side.

"That's not mine." Mercedes watched the detective slip on a pair of gloves, place the weapon in a plastic bag and seal it shut.

"It matches the make of the murder weapon. We'll have to do some testing."

"I've been setup," Mercedes said. "Someone is trying to frame me for murder."

Detective Wilson gave Mercedes a quick glance, but remained silent as he waited for the investigators to finish digging through the trash.

"The rest of the dumpster is clean, Wilson," one of them finally announced.

The men crawled out of the dumpster and began tossing the bags of trash inside.

"I need you to wait over there." Wilson pointed to the stoop before he made his way over to the crime scene van.

"I can't believe this," Mercedes groaned.

"Me neither. I never would've given them permission if I had the slightest inkling there was somethin' in the dumpster," Carlita said. "Why you? I don't get it."

"It's the perfect setup. Whoever did Jon Luis in totally set me up. They know who we are and if the cops do enough diggin' around, they're gonna put me in jail and throw away the key."

"Not if I can help it," Carlita said.

The detective slowly made his way over. "Our preliminary examination indicates that the weapon we found in your dumpster matches the weapon that killed Mr. Luis. Just between you and me, I don't think you're dumb enough to go around telling someone you shot Jon Luis and that you tossed the weapon in your dumpster."

"I'm not and I didn't."

"We'll be sending the gun in for analysis. In the meantime, please don't leave town."

"I won't," Mercedes promised. A sudden thought popped into her head. "Wait."

The detective turned.

"When did you get this so-called anonymous tip?"

"This morning, a few hours ago."

"That's interesting," Mercedes said. After he left, mother and daughter stepped inside the apartment building. "I gotta tell you something. I'll wait until we're home."

Mother and daughter tromped up the stairs and into their apartment.

Mercedes closed the door behind them. "No one in the author group knew I was back except Cricket. The others thought I was still in New York. Ma, I told Cricket everything. I was sure she wasn't Jon Luis' killer. Now I'm beginnin' to think I was wrong."

"You're sure?" Carlita asked. "A hundred percent sure she's the only one who knew you were still here in Savannah?"

"I can't be certain, but I think so. That's why I asked Detective Wilson when he received the anonymous tip. It was right around the time I stopped by *The Book Nook* and left a message for Cricket, asking her to call me. The store worker saw me. He wrote my name on a Post-it note and told me he would let her know as soon as he saw her. She called me not long after I left the bookstore."

"You're thinkin' she somehow found out you were here, brought the murder weapon by, tossed it in the dumpster and then called the cops?"

"It's the only thing that makes sense. She said she was out running some errands. Cricket knew all about George Delmario, knew all about the Madison Square / Herbert Honeycutt death."

Mercedes tapped her foot on the floor. "I'm still not sure about the Russian connection."

"Maybe it was the Russians," Carlita said. "They got nervous cuz they heard Warren Paulson was going to start pointing fingers, so they took him out. Now, years later, they're probably still workin' the area, heard Jon Luis was investigating the case and did him in."

"It could be. Some of the puzzle pieces are still missing. I'm putting Cricket at the top of the list of suspects, along with Stephanie, the romance writer, and Tom Muldoon. I don't think it was Austin. He's too young."

"Unless he's got a Russian connection."

"I doubt it," Mercedes said.

"Always suspect the least suspect," Carlita said. "What do they always talk about on those detective shows? Motive and opportunity."

"Yeah," Mercedes nodded. "Motive would be to silence Jon Luis and opportunity would be me. To set me up, someone Luis was already investigating...with mafia ties no less. I'm gonna read Jon Luis' draft again. Now that I have more of the background, I might be able to glean a few more clues. Plus, I'm gonna have to keep a close eye on the draft. I told Cricket I had it."

Carlita glanced at her watch. "I'm gonna run downstairs and check on Paulie, Gina and the kids." She opened the front door and stepped into the hall. "We better be on our guard and make sure we keep the doors locked. It's creepy knowin' this Luis' killer was in our alley, throwing a murder weapon in our dumpster."

"If it wasn't so horrifying, I think it would make a great story for one of my books," Mercedes said.

After her mother left, Mercedes began re-reading Luis' draft. Luis outlined his research in detail. She started with George Delmario's death. Mercedes had heard bits and pieces of the tale, mainly how Delmario had gone into the alley after closing his store, to take out the trash and he was gunned down in a drive-by shooting. "Sounds like a hit to me," Mercedes muttered.

Delmario died of multiple gunshot wounds. The murder weapon was never found, nor was anyone ever named as a suspect in the case. Delmario's wife, Louise, was questioned extensively, but she claimed she never heard anything, had fallen asleep waiting for her husband and didn't discover his body until the next morning.

Mercedes always suspected Delmario's wife had been warned to keep quiet or face the same fate. Instead, she quickly packed up her belongings, closed the business and headed back to New York.

Jon Luis briefly mentioned the property changed hands and was now owned by Carlita Garlucci and her family. He'd even jotted several notes about his plan to question the family to find out how they'd come to own the property since there was no trail of a traditional property sale.

Mercedes suspected that's where she came in. Jon Luis dangled the carrot, telling her he had info on the Herbert Honeycutt case when, in fact, he planned to meet her to pump her for information.

She finished reading the Delmario information and started reading his research into the Madison Square / Honeycutt murder. His theory was Teresa Honeycutt hired someone to murder her husband, intent on collecting a large insurance policy. He even alluded to the fact Honeycutt believed his wife had faked a fall, she wasn't wheelchair bound and even interviewed several close family friends.

Luis jotted notes of his planned meeting with Tierney Grant, how he knew the young woman had inherited the Honeycutt home and he hoped he would be able to search the property. Luis also suspected Tierney Grant and Teresa Honeycutt were somehow related.

What if Tierney was Jon Luis' killer? She knew he was investigating the Honeycutt case. That wouldn't be reason enough to kill the man, unless she was desperate to stop him.

Mercedes finished reading the part about Warren Paulson's Russian connection, his boating incident and how his body was never recovered.

"Was Warren Paulson murdered?" Mercedes whispered. She slid her chair back and wandered over to the window, staring out into the courtyard. At first, she thought maybe the killer knew about the book draft from Luis' publisher, but maybe not.

Luis hid the book draft in his storage unit for a reason. He had the storage unit key with him at the time of his death. What if Jon Luis had lined up two meetings the night of his death...the first one with his killer, and a second with Mercedes?

Mercedes needed to set a trap...but how? Was Cricket a killer? She seemed like such a sweet lady. Maybe she got scared when Luis started snooping around.

Knock. Knock. Mercedes hurried to the front door and peeked through the hole, certain her mother had forgotten her house keys. It was Cool Bones.

She opened the door. "Hi Cool Bones. Ma isn't here. She's downstairs."

"That's okay. I wanted to stop by on my way to practice. She slipped a note under my door, inviting me to an Italian feast here in the hall tomorrow night so I could meet Paulie's wife, Gina. She also said something about a going-away party for Elvira."

"I forgot all about it. Yeah. Ma mentioned it."

"Where is Elvira going?" Cool Bones asked.

Mercedes glanced over his shoulder at Elvira's front door. "Ma evicted her."

"And she's throwing her a going-away party?" Cool Bones chuckled.

"There's more to the story. Elvira's lease was almost up. She was moving anyway, but when the woman set her apartment on fire, it was the last straw."

"I thought I smelled smoke the other day." Cool Bones shook his head. "That woman. Once she gets a bee in her bonnet, you never know what she's gonna do. I wonder where she's moving to."

"Across the alley." Mercedes motioned to the back of the building.

"Our alley?"

"Yep. If you look out your living room window, you'll be able to see her new place."

Cool Bones let out a low whistle. "You don't say. Well, I'll be here for the dinner." He patted his stomach. "Your mother makes some mean Italian."

"Ma is a great cook," Mercedes said. "I'll be sure to let her know."

Cool Bones turned to go and then he stopped. "Oh. I almost forgot to tell you. After wrapping up my gig down at the Thirsty Crow this morning, I was walking home and I noticed someone up ahead of me, so I kinda hung back. You never know what kinda characters are lurking around at three in the morning. I followed the person all the way here and watched as they turned down our alley and walked to the other end. They were doing something over by the dumpster. I thought maybe it was a homeless person, but they didn't start digging around in the trash. It looked like they dropped something inside and then they took off."

Chapter 20

"The person was on foot?" Mercedes asked.

"Yes ma'am. At least as far as I could see. Course, they coulda parked somewhere and walked."

"Someone called in an anonymous tip to the police this morning, saying that a gun used in a shooting down by the river was in our dumpster."

"I heard something about a man's body being found down by the river on the news the other day," Cool Bones said. "Why would the gun be in our dumpster?"

"Because I was the one who found his body," Mercedes said. She didn't go into detail and Cool Bones didn't ask. "What time did you say this happened? Were you able to tell if the person was a man or a woman?"

"It was around 3:00, maybe closer to 3:15 this morning, right after the bar closed. It was too dark to see anything. I'm sorry Mercedes. I wish I could help. I best be goin' on to my practice. If I think of anything else, I'll let you know." Cool Bones tipped his hat, trekked down the steps and out the door.

Mercedes watched him leave. What if the killer grew suspicious when Mercedes suddenly left town and Autumn joined the group?

What if Jon Luis hadn't connected the dots? What if he told his publisher what he was working on? Still, Luis had a reason for hiding the draft in his storage unit, more than likely because his apartment had been ransacked.

Mercedes wandered into her bedroom and plopped down in the chair. She slid the manuscript out of the plastic bag and spotted a small oblong object she hadn't noticed before.

"What is this?" She tipped the bag upside down and the small object fell into her hand. It was a

USB flash drive. Mercedes' fingers trembled as she wiggled the device into the USB port on the side of her laptop and clicked to open the drive. Her eyes scanned the list and she found a folder named MIS Manuscript.

Mercedes double-clicked on the heading and Jon Luis' manuscript popped up on the screen. She studied the online manuscript. It was identical to the hard copy she'd been reading, except for the cover page. It listed the publisher as Live Oak Publishing.

She grabbed her phone, tapped the camera icon and scrolled through the pictures she'd taken of the books by JL Cordele they'd found in Jon Luis' storage unit. The publisher listed on those was The Batton Group.

"Why didn't I think of this before? Jon Luis began writing under another name and at the same time, switched publishers." Mercedes set the phone on the desk and typed Austin Crawford, author.

The majority of Austin's books were published under Crawford Publishing Company, except for a non-fiction book, featuring tips on how to research local history. It was published under Garnett Publishing and Mercedes vaguely recognized the name.

Carlita popped her head inside Mercedes' bedroom door. "I'm back."

"Great," Mercedes said. "I'm just doin' some more research." She began researching Cricket's books, all published under Learner Crafts Publishing and another publisher Mercedes didn't recognize.

She moved on to Tom Muldoon. There were several pages of thriller/suspense books written under his name and most were with a major publisher, Barnette Book Group. Tom's newest book, *The Last to Fall,* was ranking well and published under the name Tom Muldoon with no publishing credits. She clicked on another of his books, *Fight the Calm,* and almost hit the floor when she spotted Live Oak Publishing on the second page.

"It's Tom," Mercedes leaned back in her chair as she stared at the words. Tom and Jon Luis had used the same publishing company. Had Tom murdered Jon Luis and set Mercedes up? If so, why?

Mercedes opened a second browser and typed in Warren Paulson, Savannah, Georgia. Several old news articles popped up about Paulson's case. One article reported he'd gone missing and was presumed to have died in a boating mishap.

"I'm missing something," Mercedes groaned. She began to study the online manuscript, all of which was identical to the handwritten one, minus the notes Jon Luis had jotted on the side. At the very bottom was a single, additional paragraph that she missed on her first scan of Jon Luis' draft book.

Warren Paulson wasn't murdered and he didn't die in a boating accident. Follow the money.

"Follow the money," Mercedes said. "The money that Warren Paulson was paid for selling satellite information to the Russians. What happened to it?" She slid out of the chair and wandered over to the window, staring out into the courtyard. "If I had a bunch of money, I might invest it, stick it in an overseas bank account or...buy property."

She darted back to her chair. Mercedes' fingers flew over the keyboard as she searched the Board of Assessor's website for property owned by Warren Paulson. The site listed a property with several acres and a single family home, purchased by Warren Paulson several years ago.

At the bottom of the sheet was an additional link and Mercedes clicked on it. It was a quitclaim deed. The property that Warren

Paulson purchased changed hands and was now owned by Tom Muldoon!

Mercedes' mind whirled. Why would Warren Paulson deed his property to Tom Muldoon unless... "Oh my gosh!"

"Ma!"

Carlita ran into the room. "What?"

"I think Tom Muldoon knew someone who worked at Live Oak Publishing. That person mentioned Luis' new book to Muldoon and the cases he was investigating. Muldoon tracked down Jon Luis and discovered he was researching not only George Delmario's death but also the deaths of Herbert Honeycutt and Warren Paulson."

"Yeah? How do they link to Tom Muldoon?" Carlita asked.

"Warren Paulson was a Russian informant. Rumors began to circulate. He was getting pressure from the feds and threats from the

Russians, so he staged his disappearance in a boating mishap." Mercedes said. "But he didn't die. He went into hiding and, at some point in time, he changed his identity. Warren Paulson, Russian informant, became Tom Muldoon, mystery and thriller writer."

Mercedes would bet money Muldoon was the one who mentioned Jon Luis to the author group. Perhaps he was even the one who told Jon Luis about Mercedes, how she lived in the infamous George Delmario / mafia house and put the bug in Mercedes' ear to contact Jon Luis.

He orchestrated their meeting, without either of them knowing it. Muldoon lured Jon Luis to the riverfront, maybe even confronted him about the book research and then murdered him, knowing Mercedes was on her way to meet with Jon Luis.

How could she prove it? Unless...she turned the tables and lured Tom Muldoon into a trap.

Mercedes grabbed her phone and dialed Detective Wilson's number.

"Hello Ms. Garlucci. We don't have the results back on the gun yet."

"That's not why I'm calling. One of our tenants stopped by earlier to tell me he watched someone drop something into our dumpster around 3:15 this morning and I think I know who not only planted the gun, but also who murdered Jon Luis and set me up."

"You've been busy," Wilson said. "I hope you're not breaking the law."

"No, at least not yet. I'm working on setting a trap and I need your help." She laid out her theory to Wilson in detail, telling him she planned to use the rough draft of the book as bait and was certain that Tom Muldoon, aka Warren Paulson, would fall for it. "I did obtain the book draft under questionable circumstances that I'd rather not discuss."

She explained how she linked Muldoon and Jon Luis' books to the same publisher and that Warren Paulson's property was quitclaimed to Tom Muldoon.

"Jon Luis was hot on Muldoon's trail. I think Muldoon somehow found out about Jon Luis' research, which included George Delmario, the previous owner of our property. Muldoon brought up Jon Luis during one of our author meetings and covertly worked behind the scenes to tell Jon Luis about me and vice versa. It was the perfect setup; get rid of Jon Luis and I would take the fall."

"What is your plan?" the detective asked.

"I'm gonna tell the author group I think there's a Russian connection, maybe someone with connections to Warren Paulson's case. If my plan works, Luis' killer will hear I have Luis' manuscript that I'm onto something and come after it."

"You want to lure a potential killer to your property?" Detective Wilson asked.

"The killer is already lurking around," Mercedes said, "although it wouldn't hurt if you could send a few extra patrol cars around here tonight."

The detective sighed heavily. "I think it's a mistake, but I can't stop you. I hope you know what you're getting yourself into."

"I think I do. Now all I have to do is convince my brothers to help me out."

***

"Hi Cricket. Yeah, it's me, Mercedes. I think I hit the jackpot."

"No. I'm not holding a winning lottery ticket. It's something better." Mercedes pressed the speaker button so her family could hear. "I finished reading Luis' manuscript again, the one he was working on when he was murdered.

Believe it or not, I think I figured out who killed him."

"Seriously?" Cricket asked. "Who is it?"

"I can't say yet, other than there's a Russian connection. I have a little more digging around to do tonight and then I plan to take the manuscript to the police first thing in the morning. The manuscript links to a property deal that links the killer to Luis. In the meantime, I'm locking it up downstairs in the pawnshop for safekeeping."

"Unbelievable," Cricket said. "Wait until the others in our group hear this."

"You better keep it on the down low for now," Mercedes said. "I'm still puttin' the pieces together, but if I'm on the right track, it's gonna blow Jon Luis' murder case wide open."

They chatted for a few more minutes, with Mercedes assuring Cricket she would be at the next author meeting and then told her good-bye before slipping the phone into her back pocket. "It's a done deal. If Tom Muldoon is Luis' killer, the same man who set me up, he'll be here tonight, trying to get his hands on this manuscript."

"How can you be sure?" Tony asked. "You told this Cricket person not to say anything."

"Asking Cricket to keep a secret is like trying to stay dry while you're swimming in the ocean," Mercedes said. "It ain't gonna happen. The other three will hear that I have Jon Luis' manuscript within the hour," she predicted.

The rest of the evening crawled by as Mercedes waited for the pawnshop to close. The family ate early and Gina and the kids stayed in Carlita and Mercedes' apartment while Mercedes and her brothers headed downstairs to guard the pawnshop.

"We need to arm ourselves." Tony stepped over to the desk and unlocked the top left-hand drawer. "What kind of gun you want Paulie?"

"Whatever you wanna give me."

Tony handed him a Ruger. "It's already loaded."

"You keep these things loaded?"

"Yeah. If someone decides to rob the pawnshop, they're not gonna wait for me to load my gun."

"True."

"What about you Mercedes?" Paulie asked.

"I got my own." Mercedes pulled a small silver gun with a pearl handle out of her jacket pocket.

"That looks familiar." Tony pointed at the gun.

"Ma and I found it in Pop's safe not long after his death."

"Ah." Tony pulled out a gun, checked the chamber to make sure it was loaded and then shut the desk drawer. "Paulie, you take the back hall. I'll take the front of the store."

"What about me?" Mercedes asked.

"You stay here, behind the counter where it's safest. If this thug shows up, he'll have to get through Paulie or me before he gets to ya. If anything happens, call the cops."

Mercedes smiled. "I swear I have the best bros in the whole world."

"Yeah, well don't be passin' out the compliments just yet. It's gonna be a long night."

Tony killed the lights and crept to the front of the store while Paulie made his way to the back. Mercedes eased into the desk chair and glanced at the glowing hands on the wall clock. It was only ten and Tony was right, it was going be a long night.

She stayed in the back area for what seemed like forever, getting up every fifteen minutes to stretch her legs and check on her brothers. They agreed to leave the store's back door ajar, just in case, to keep the lines of communication open.

Around midnight, she dozed off.

"Mercedes," Tony hissed in her ear.

Mercedes jerked upright, her arms flailing in the air. "What?"

"I'm gonna take a quick bathroom break. Keep an eye out front."

"Sure." Mercedes wiggled out of the chair and walked around the side of the counter.

Click...click.

"Did you hear that?" she whispered.

Tony nodded and held a finger to his lips. He slipped past Mercedes and motioned her to move back as he crept toward the front of the store.

She could see the shadow of someone in front of the door and then it faded. Moments later, Paulie raced into the room motioning wildly toward the hall.

Tony ran past his sister. "Stay here in case there's more than one."

Mercedes ducked behind the counter. She gripped her gun in one hand and her cell phone in the other. Her heart began to race when she heard the tinkle of glass breaking. Then silence. All she could hear was the sound of her heart pounding in her ears.

Ugh. She heard a loud grunt, followed by a loud thump.

"Call the cops!" Paulie shouted.

Mercedes' fingers shook as she dialed 911. "Yes. This is Mercedes Garlucci, 210 Mulberry Street in Savannah. Someone is trying to break into our pawnshop."

"A patrol car is on the way," the dispatcher said. "They're only three minutes out."

"Thank you." She disconnected the call and ran into the hall where Paulie had Tom Muldoon pinned to the floor. Tony was standing over him, his gun pointed at Muldoon's head.

The sound of sirens filled the air and Mercedes ran to the back door to let the police inside. Two patrol cars screeched to a halt in the alley and officers sprang from the car. "We got a guy inside who was trying to rob our store," Mercedes said breathlessly.

While the officers ran inside to assist Mercedes' brothers, Mercedes dialed Detective Skip Wilson's cell phone.

"Detective Skip Wilson speaking."

"This is Mercedes Garlucci. I think we've got Jon Luis' killer."

Chapter 21

"Hold the door, Mercedes." Carlita grabbed a couple of potholders and carried the bubbling tagliatelle pasta dish out of the apartment and to the table in the hall. She carefully set it next to the other two pasta dishes she'd pulled from the oven.

Cool Bones' apartment door opened and he stepped into the hall. "I thought I smelled something heavenly." He took a breath and closed his eyes. "I've been saving my appetite all day for this."

"I'm glad you could make it," Carlita said. "Grab a seat."

Elvira's apartment door opened and she met Cool Bones' gaze. "Well hello tall, dark and handsome." She batted her eyes and plunked down in the chair next to him.

Cool Bones grinned, displaying a gleaming set of pearly whites. "Hello Elvira. Have you finished moving out?"

"Almost. All I've got left to move is my bed. Would you like to help?"

Mercedes snorted. "Ha."

"I-uh. Well, if you want to move it tonight, I can see if Tony and Paulie want to add a little muscle. We can get it over to your new place in one trip."

Elvira frowned. "That wasn't what I had in mind."

Shelby and Violet emerged from their apartment, saving Cool Bones from having to reply. "I hope we're not late."

"Not at all," Carlita said. "I'm still waitin' on the others. They're closing up shop now."

Gina and the kids stepped out of Tony's apartment and climbed the stairs. "It looks like you outdone yourself Ma." Gina herded the kids to the other side of the table and then followed Carlita into the apartment to grab the plates, napkins and silverware.

They finished setting the table and Tony and Paulie joined them. "These smells have been torturing me all afternoon," Tony said.

After everyone was seated, they passed around the pasta dishes, baskets brimming with garlic rolls and a large bowl of salad.

Carlita took her seat at the head of the table and a slow smile spread across her face as she gazed at her children and grandchildren. The only ones missing were her Vinnies...her husband and oldest son.

A twinge of sadness washed over Carlita and she forced it from her mind.

During a lull in the conversation, Cool Bones asked how the Jon Luis' murder investigation was going.

"It's over," Mercedes said.

"Mercedes set a trap for the killer and he walked right into it," Carlita said.

"Or broke into it," Paulie quipped. "As in, tried to break into the pawnshop, but we were waitin' for him."

"Tom Muldoon ain't no match for the Garlucci brothers," Tony bragged.

"Did he confess to killing Jon Luis?" Elvira asked.

"No, but I think the authorities are close to having enough evidence to charge him. They're holding him in jail on a technicality right now. One of the publishers at Live Oak admitted he let Tom Muldoon take a look at Jon Luis' draft. They were friends from way back."

"Mercedes figured Muldoon became suspicious of Autumn attending the author group when she showed up and Mercedes didn't," Carlita explained. "When Autumn started nosing around, asking questions about publishers, Muldoon decided to ramp up his plan to frame Mercedes by tossing the murder weapon into our dumpster and then he made an anonymous phone call to the police."

"Thank God Cool Bones saw someone toss something into our dumpster on his way home from work," Mercedes said. "The killer who wrote thrillers."

Elvira elbowed Cool Bones. "If I were you, I'd ask for a discount on this month's rent."

"Elvira," Carlita warned.

"What?"

"That's something you would pull."

"Well, soon enough, I'll be out of your hair forever."

"You're moving across the alley," Mercedes said.

"Yeah, but it's not like living under the same roof."

"Close enough," Carlita muttered.

Elvira straightened her shoulders. "I think you're going to miss me, probably even beg me to move back in. I'm not gonna do it, so you might as well start looking for a new tenant now that the repairs to the apartment are done."

"I think I'm gonna put it off for a few weeks and enjoy the peace and quiet," Carlita said.

"When you do, make sure you go over the applicants with a fine tooth comb," Elvira said. "Quality tenants like me are few and far between."

"There's only one Elvira Cobb."

"I can't argue with you there," Carlita said.

The end.

If you enjoyed reading "Setup in Savannah," please take a moment to leave a review. It would be greatly appreciated. Thank you.

The series continues...book 8 in the "Made in Savannah" series coming soon!

Save 50-90% on Your Next Cozy Mystery

https://hopecallaghan.com/hope-callaghan-books-on-sale/

List of Hope Callaghan Books

Audiobooks
(On Sale Now or FREE with Audible Trial)

Key to Savannah: Book 1 (Made in Savannah Series)
Road to Savannah: Book 2 (Made in Savannah Series)
Justice in Savannah: Book 3 (Made in Savannah Series)

Cozy Mystery Collections

Hope Callaghan Cozy Mysteries: Collection (1st in Series Edition)

Made in Savannah Cozy Mystery Series

Key to Savannah: Book 1
Road to Savannah: Book 2
Justice in Savannah: Book 3
Swag in Savannah: Book 4
Trouble in Savannah: Book 5
Missing in Savannah: Book 6
Setup in Savannah: Book 7
Book 8: Coming Soon!

Garden Girls Cozy Mystery Series

Who Murdered Mr. Malone? Book 1
Grandkids Gone Wild: Book 2
Smoky Mountain Mystery: Book 3
Death by Dumplings: Book 4
Eye Spy: Book 5
Magnolia Mansion Mysteries: Book 6
Missing Milt: Book 7
Bully in the 'Burbs: Book 8
Fall Girl: Book 9
Home for the Holidays: Book 10
Sun, Sand, and Suspects: Book 11
Look Into My Ice: Book 12
Forget Me Knot: Book 13
Nightmare in Nantucket: Book 14
Greed with Envy: Book 15
Dying for Dollars: Book 16
Stranger Among Us: Book 17
Book 18: Coming Soon!
Garden Girls Box Set I – (Books 1-3)
Garden Girls Box Set II – (Books 4-6)
Garden Girls Box Set III – (Books 7-9)

Cruise Ship Cozy Mystery Series

Starboard Secrets: Book 1
Portside Peril: Book 2
Lethal Lobster: Book 3
Deadly Deception: Book 4

Vanishing Vacationers: Book 5
Cruise Control: Book 6
Killer Karaoke: Book 7
Suite Revenge: Book 8
Cruisin' for a Bruisin': Book 9
High Seas Heist: Book 10
Book 11: Coming Soon!
Cruise Ship Cozy Mysteries Box Set I (Books 1-3)
Cruise Ship Cozy Mysteries Box Set II (Books 4-6)

Sweet Southern Sleuths Cozy Mysteries Short Stories Series

Teepees and Trailer Parks: Book 1
Bag of Bones: Book 2
Southern Stalker: Book 3
Two Settle the Score: Book 4
Killer Road Trip: Book 5
Pups in Peril: Book 6
Dying To Get Married-In: Book 7
Deadly Drive-In: Book 8
Secrets of a Stranger: Book 9
Library Lockdown: Book 10
Vandals & Vigilantes: Book 11
Fatal Frolic: Book 12
Sweet Southern Sleuths Box Set I: (Books 1-4)
Sweet Southern Sleuths Box Set: II: (Books 5-8)
Sweet Southern Sleuths Box Set III: (Books 9-12)
Sweet Southern Sleuths 12 Book Box Set (Entire Series)

Samantha Rite Deception Mystery Series

Waves of Deception: Book 1
Winds of Deception: Book 2
Tides of Deception: Book 3
Samantha Rite Series Box Set – (Books 1-3-The Complete Series)

Get Free eBooks and More

Sign up for my Free Cozy Mysteries Newsletter to get free and discounted books, giveaways & soon-to-be-released books!

hopecallaghan.com/newsletter

Meet the Author

Hope Callaghan is an author who loves to write Christian books, especially Christian Mystery and Cozy Mystery books. She has written more than 50 mystery books (and counting) in five series.

In March 2017, Hope won a Mom's Choice Award for her book, "Key to Savannah," Book 1 in the Made in Savannah Cozy Mystery Series.

Born and raised in a small town in West Michigan, she now lives in Florida with her husband.

She is the proud mother of one daughter and a stepdaughter and stepson. When she's not doing the thing she loves best - writing books - she enjoys cooking, traveling and reading books.

Hope loves to connect with her readers! Connect with her today!

Visit hopecallaghan.com for special offers, free books, and soon-to-be-released books!

Email: hope@hopecallaghan.com

Facebook:
https://www.facebook.com/hopecallaghanauthor/

Fresh Pasta Dough Recipe

INGREDIENTS:

1 ½ cups flour

½ cup semolina flour (pasta flour)

2 whole eggs, at room temperature

3 egg yolks, at room temperature

DIRECTIONS:

In a large bowl, whisk together the flour and the semolina. Create a well in the center and add the eggs and egg yolks. Using a fork, break up the eggs then gradually start to draw flour from the edges of the well into the mixture.

If the dough gets too firm to mix with the fork switch to mixing with your hands. Continue to work in flour until the dough no longer sticks to your hands; you may not need to incorporate all of the flour. (I used a bit more than what the recipe called for.)

Transfer the dough to a lightly floured surface and knead the dough for 8 to 10 minutes or until it is smooth and pliable. Wrap the dough tightly in plastic wrap and allow to rest for at least 30 minutes.

If using a pasta roller: Divide the dough into 4 pieces. Starting with the machine set to the widest setting, pass the dough through the rollers. Fold the dough into thirds and pass it through again 2 more times. Continue passing the pasta through the machine, reducing the setting a few notches each time. You may need to dust a bit with flour if the dough sticks to the rollers at all. Once you reach your desired thickness, use the cutting attachment to cut the pasta sheet into fettuccine. Dust the cut pasta with more flour to prevent sticking and repeat with the remaining dough.

If using a rolling pin: Divide the dough in half. Dust your surface with flour and sprinkle generously on your rolling pin.

*Roll out the dough as thin and as evenly possible, adding flour as needed to prevent sticking. Use a paring knife (a pizza cutter works great!) to cut your dough into even ribbons, then set aside, dusting the cut pasta with more flour. Repeat with the remaining dough. (At this point, the pasta can be transferred to a sealable plastic bag and frozen for up to 3 months; do not defrost before cooking.)

Cook the pasta in a large pot of generously salted boiling water, checking for doneness after just 1 minute; fresh pasta cooks very quickly. As soon as it is al dente, no more than 3 or 4 minutes, drain, reserving some of the cooking water if desired for saucing the pasta. Toss with your sauce, loosen with some of the reserved cooking water as needed and serve immediately.

*Note: You must get the dough as thin as possible and cut them into small strips, otherwise, it will be too thick and end up having the texture of dumplings.

Garlucci Family Secret Pasta Sauce Recipe

Ingredients:
2 tablespoons olive oil
1 onion, chopped
4 cloves garlic, minced
1-1/2 cups pureed tomatoes
1-1/2 tablespoon tomato paste
2 tablespoons fresh basil, chopped
1 teaspoon black pepper
1/2 teaspoon salt
1-1/4 cup heavy cream
1/2 cup grated parmesan cheese
3/4 pound fettuccine

Directions:
Heat olive oil in a pan on medium heat. Add onions and garlic. Cook until tender about 3 minutes.
Add in tomato paste and pureed tomato, stir.
Season with basil, black pepper and salt.
Stir until everything is blended.
Add the heavy cream and let it simmer for about 5 minutes until the sauce thickens.
Add cooked pasta.
After plated, sprinkle with parmesan cheese.

Made in United States
Orlando, FL
02 November 2023